Raven

V.C. ANDREWS®

Raven

G.K. Hall & Co. • Chivers Press
Thorndike, Maine   Bath, England

This Large Print edition is published by G.K. Hall & Co., USA and by Chivers Press, England.

Published in 1999 in the U.S. by arrangement with Pocket Books, a division of Simon & Schuster, Inc.

Published in 1999 in the U.K. by arrangement with Simon & Schuster Ltd.

U.S. Hardcover 0-7838-0330-3 (Core Series Edition)
U.K. Hardcover 0-7540-1235-2 (Windsor Large Print)

The text of this Large Print edition is unabridged.
Other aspects of the book may vary from the original edition.
Set in 16 .pt. Plantin.
Printed in the United States on permanent paper.

British Library Cataloguing in Publication Data available

Library of Congress Cataloging in Publication Data

Andrews, V. C. (Virginia C.)
    Raven / V.C. Andrews.
      p.   cm.
    ISBN 0-7838-0330-3 (lg. print : hc : alk. paper)
    1. Large type books.   I. Title.
[PS3551.N454R37   1999]
813'.54—dc21   98-39757

Raven

Prologue

"I never asked to be born," I threw back at my mother when she complained about all the trouble I had caused her from the day I was born. The school had called, and the truancy officer had threatened to take Mama to court if I stayed home one more time. I hated my school. It was a hive of snobs buzzing around this queen bee or that and threatening to sting me if I so much as tried to enter their precious little social circles. My classes were so big most of my teachers didn't even know I existed anyway! If it wasn't for the new automated homeroom cards, no one would know I hadn't gone to school.

Mama kicked the refrigerator door closed with her bare foot and slapped a bottle of beer down so hard on the counter it almost shattered. She tore off the cap with her opener and stared at me, her eyes bloodshot. The truancy officer's phone call had jolted her out of a dead sleep. She brought the bottle to her lips and sucked on it, the muscles in her thin neck pulsating with the effort to get as much down her throat as she could in one gulp. Then she glared at me again. I saw she had a bruise on the bottom of her right forearm and a scraped elbow.

We were having one of those Indian summers. The temperature had reached ninety today, and it was nearly October twenty-first. Mama's hair, just as black as mine, hung limply over her cheeks. Her bangs were too long and uneven. She pushed her lower lip out and blew up to sweep the strands out of her eyes. Once, she had been a very pretty woman with eyes that glittered like black pearls. She had a richly dark complexion with distinct, high cheekbones and perfect facial features. Women shot silicone into their lips to get the shape and fullness Mama's had naturally. I used to be flattered when people compared me to her in those days. All I ever dreamed of being was as pretty as my mother.

Now, I pretended I wasn't even related to her. Sometimes, I pretended she wasn't even there.

"How am I supposed to scratch out a living and watch a twelve-year-old, too? They should be giving me medals, not threats."

Mama's way of scratching out a living was working as a barmaid at a dump called

Charlie Boy's in Newburgh, New York. Some nights, she didn't come home until nearly four in the morning, long after the bar had closed. If she wasn't drunk, she was high on something and would go stumbling around our one-bedroom apartment, knocking into furniture and dropping things.

I slept on the pullout couch, so I usually woke up or heard her, but I always pretended I was still asleep. I hated talking to her when she was in that condition. Sometimes, I could smell her before I heard her. It was as if she had soaked her clothing in whiskey and beer.

Mama looked much older than her thirty-one years now. She had dark shadows under her eyes and wrinkles that looked like lines drawn with an eyebrow pencil at the corners. Her rich complexion had turned into a pasty, pale yellow, and her once silky hair looked like a mop made of piano wire. It was streaked with premature gray strands and always looked dirty and stringy to me.

Mama smoked and drank and didn't seem to care what man she went out with as long as he was willing to pay for what she wanted. I stopped keeping track of their names. Their faces had begun to merge into one, their red eyes peering at me with vague interest. Usually, I was just as much of a surprise to them as they were to me.

"You never said you had a daughter," most would remark.

Mama would shrug and reply, "Oh, didn't I? Well, I do. You have a problem with that?"

Some didn't say anything; some said no or shook their heads and laughed.

"You're the one with the problem," one man told her. That put her into a tirade about my father.

We rarely talked about him. Mama would say only that he was a handsome Latino but a disappointment when it came to living up to his responsibilities.

"As are most men," she warned me.

She got me to believe that my real father's promises were like rainbows, beautiful while they lingered in the air but soon fading until they were only vague memories. And there was never a pot of gold! He would never come back, and he would never send us anything.

As long as I could remember, we lived in this small apartment in a building that looked as if a strong wind could knock it over. The walls in the corridors were chipped and gouged in places, as if some maddened creature had tried to dig its way out. The outside walls were scarred with graffiti, and the walkway was shattered so that there was just dirt in many sections where cement once had been. The small patch of lawn between the building and the street had turned sour years ago. The grass was a sickly pale green, and there was so much garbage in it that no one could run a lawn mower over it.

The sinks in our apartment always gave us trouble, dripping or clogging. I couldn't even guess how many times the toilet had overflowed. The tub was full of rust around the drain, and the shower dripped and usually ran out of hot water before I could finish or wash my hair. I know we had lots of mice, because I was always finding their droppings in drawers or under dressers and tables. Sometimes, I could hear them scurrying about, and a few times I saw one before it scurried under a piece of furniture. We put out traps and caught a couple, but for every one we trapped, there were ten to take its place.

Mama was always promising to get us out. A new apartment was just around the corner, just as soon as she saved another hundred for the deposit. But I knew that if she did get any spare money, she would spend it on whiskey, beer, or pot. One of her new boyfriends introduced her to cocaine, and she had some of that occasionally, but usually it was too expensive for her.

We had a television set that often lost its picture. I could get it back sometimes by knocking it hard on the side. Sometimes, Mama received a welfare check. I never understood why she did or didn't. She cursed the system and complained when there wasn't a check. If I got to it first, I would cash it at my mom's friend's convenience store, and get us some good groceries and some clothes for myself. If I didn't, she hid it or doled out some money to me in small dribs and drabs, and I had to make do with it.

I knew that other kids my age would steal what they couldn't afford, but that wasn't for me. There was a girl in my building, Lila Thomas, who went with some other girls from across town on weekends and raided malls. She had been caught shoplifting, but she didn't seem afraid of being caught again. She made fun of me all the time because I wouldn't go along. She called me "the girl scout" and told everyone I would end up selling cookies for a living.

I didn't care about not having her as a close friend. Most of the time, I was happy being with myself, reading a magazine or watching soaps whenever I could get the television set to work. I tried not to think about Mama sleeping late, maybe even with some new man in her room. I had gotten so I could look through people and pretend they weren't even there.

"You just better damn well go to school tomorrow, Raven. I don't need no government people coming around here and snooping," she muttered, and wiped strands of hair away from her cheek. "You listening to me?"

"Yes," I said.

She stared hard and drank some more of her beer. It was only nine-fifteen in the morning. I hated the taste of beer anyway, but just the thought of drinking it this early made my stomach churn. Mama suddenly realized what day it was and that I should be in school now, too. Her eyes popped.

"Why are you home today?" she cried.

"I had a stomachache," I said. "I'm getting my period. That's what the nurse told me in school when I had cramps and left class."

She looked at me with a cold glint in her dark eyes and nodded.

"Welcome to hell," she said. "You'll soon understand why parents give thanks when they have a boy. Men have it so much easier.

You better watch yourself now," she warned, pointing the neck of the beer bottle at me.

"What do you mean?"

"What do I mean?" she mimicked. "I mean, if you got your period coming, you could get pregnant, Raven, and I won't be taking care of no baby, not me."

"I'm not getting pregnant, Mama," I said sharply.

She laughed. "That's what I said, and look at what happened."

"Well, why did you have me then?" I fired back at her. I was tired of hearing what a burden I was. I wasn't. I was the one who kept the apartment livable, cleaning up after her drunken rages, washing dishes, washing clothes, mopping the bathroom floors. I was the one who bought us food and cooked for us half the time. Sometimes, she brought food home from the restaurant, when she remembered, but it was usually cold and greasy by the time she got it home.

"Why'd I have you? Why'd I have you?" she muttered, and looked dazed, as if the question was too hard to answer. Her face brightened with rage. "I'll tell you why. Because your macho Cuban father was going to make us a home. He was positive you were going to be a boy. How could he have anything but boys? Not Mr. Macho. Then, when you were born . . .”

“What?” I asked quickly. Getting her to tell me anything about my father or what things were like for her in those days was as hard as getting top government secrets.

“He ran. As soon as he set eyes on you, he grimaced ugly and said, ‘It’s a girl? Can’t be mine.’ And he ran. Ain’t heard from him since,” she muttered. She looked thoughtful for a moment and then turned back to me. “Let that be a lesson to you about men.”

What lesson? I wondered. How did she think it made me feel to learn that my father couldn’t stand the sight of me, that my very birth sent him away? How did she think it made me feel to hear almost every day that she never asked to have me? Sometimes, she called me her punishment. I was God’s way of getting back at her, but what did she consider her sin? Not drinking or doing drugs or slumming about — oh, no. Her sin was trusting a man. Was she right? Was that the way all men would behave? Most of my mother’s friends agreed with her about men, and many of my friends, who came from homes not much better than mine, had similar ideas taught to them by their mothers.

I felt more alone than ever. Getting older,

developing as a woman, looking older than I was, all of it didn't make me feel more independent and stronger as much as it reminded me I really had no one but myself. I had many questions. I had lots of things troubling me, things a girl would want to ask her mother, but I was afraid to ask mine, and most of the time, I didn't think she could think clearly enough to answer them anyway.

"You got what you need?" she asked, dropping the empty beer bottle into the garbage.

"What do you mean?"

"What I mean is something to wear for protection. Didn't that school nurse tell you what you need?"

"Yes, Mama, I have what I need," I said. I didn't.

What I needed was a real mother and a real father, for starters, but that was something I'd see only on television.

"I don't want to hear about you not going to school, Raven. If I do, I'm going to call your uncle Reuben," she warned. She often used her brother as a threat. She knew I never liked him, never liked being in his company. I didn't think his own children liked him, and I knew my aunt Clara was afraid of him. I could see it in her eyes.

Mama returned to her bedroom and went back to sleep. I sat by the window and looked down at the street. Our apartment was on the third floor. There were no elevators, just a windy stairway that sounded as if it was about to collapse, especially when younger children ran down the steps or when Mr. Winecoup, the man who lived above us, walked up. He easily weighed three hundred pounds. The ceiling shook when he paced about in his apartment.

I looked beyond the street, out toward the mountains in the distance, and wondered what was beyond them. I dreamed of running off to find a place where the sun always shone, where houses were clean and smelled fresh, where parents laughed and loved their children, where there were fathers who cared and mothers who cared.

You might as well live in Disneyland, a voice told me. *Stop dreaming.*

I rose and began my day of solitude, finding something to eat, watching some television, waiting for Mama to wake so we could talk about dinner before she went off to her job. When she was rested and sobered up enough, she would sit before her vanity mirror and work on her hair and face enough to give others the illusion she was healthy and still attractive. While she did her makeup, she ranted and raved about her life and what she could have been if she hadn't fallen for the first good-looking man and believed his lies.

I tried to ask her questions about her own youth, but she hated answering questions about her family. Her parents had practically disowned her, and she had left home when she was eighteen, but she didn't realize any of her own dreams. The biggest and most exciting thing in her life was her small flirtation with becoming a model. Some department store manager had hired her to model in the women's department. "But then he wanted sexual favors, so I left," she told me. Once again, she went into one of her tirades about men.

"If you hate men so much," I asked her, "why do you go out with one almost every other night?"

"Don't have a smart mouth, Raven," she fired back. She thought a moment and then shrugged. "I'm entitled to some fun, aren't I? Well? I work hard. Let them take me out and spend some money on me."

"Don't you ever want to meet anyone nice, Mama?" I asked. "Don't you ever want to get married again?"

She stared at herself in the mirror. Her eyes looked sad for a moment, and then she put on that angry look and spun on me.

"*No!* I don't want to have no man lording over me again. And besides," she said, practically screaming, "I didn't get married. I never had a wedding, not even in a court."

"But I thought . . . my father . . ."

"He was your father, but he wasn't my husband. We just lived together," she said. She looked away.

"But I have his name . . . Flores," I stuttered.

"It was just to save my reputation," she admitted. She turned to me and smiled coldly. "You can call yourself whatever you want."

I stared, my heart quivering. I didn't even have a name?

When I looked in the mirror, whom did I see? No one, I thought.

I might as well be invisible, I concluded, and returned to my seat by the window, watching the gray clouds twirl toward the mountains, toward the promise of something better.

That promise.

It was all I had.

1

A Rude
Awakening

I woke to the sound of knocking, but I wasn't
sure if it was someone at our door. People
pounded on the walls in this apartment
building at all times of the day or night. The
knocking grew sharper, more frenzied, and
then I heard my uncle Reuben's voice.

"Raven, damn it, wake up. Raven!"

He hit the door so hard I thought his fist
had gone through. I reached for my robe
and got up quickly.

"Mama!" I called.

I ground the sleep from my eyes and listened. I thought I remembered hearing her
come home, but the nights were so mixed
up and confused in my memory, I wasn't
sure. "Mama?"

Uncle Reuben pounded on the door again, shaking the whole frame. I hurried to Mama's bedroom and gazed in. She wasn't there.

"Raven! Wake up!"

"Coming," I cried, and hurried to the door. When I unlocked it, he shoved it open so fast he almost knocked me over.

"What's wrong?" I demanded.

We had a small naked bulb in the hallway which turned the dirty, shadowy walls into a brown the color of a wet paper bag. There was just enough light behind Uncle Reuben to silhouette his six-foot-three-inch, stocky body. He hovered in the doorway like some bird of prey, and the silence that followed his urgency frightened me even more. He seemed to be gasping for breath as if he had run up the stairs.

"What do you want?" I cried.

"Get some things together," he ordered. "You got to come with me."

"What? Why?" I stepped back and embraced myself. I would have hated going anywhere with him in broad daylight, much less late at night.

"Put on some light," he commanded.

I found the switch and lit up the kitchen. The illumination revealed his swollen, sweaty red face, the crests of his cheeks as red as a rash. His dark eyes looked about frantically. He wore only a soiled T-shirt and a pair of oily-looking jeans. Even though he had an administrative job now with the highway department, he still had the bulky muscular frame he had built working on the road crew. His dark brown hair was cut military short, which made his ears look like the wings on Mercury's head. I used to wonder how Mama and Uncle Reuben could be siblings. His facial features were large and pronounced, the only real resemblance being in their eyes.

"What is it?" I asked. "Why are you here?"

"Not because I want to be, believe me," he replied, and went to the sink to pour himself a glass of water. "Your mother's in jail," he added.

"What?"

I had to wait for him to take long gulps of water. He put the glass in the sink as if he expected the maid would clean up after him and turned to me. For a moment, he just drank me in. His gaze made me feel as if a cold wind had slipped under my robe. I actually shivered.

"Why is Mama in jail?"

"She got picked up with some drug dealer. She's in big-time, real trouble this time," he said. "You got to come live with us in the meantime, maybe forever," he added, and spit into the sink.

"Live with you?" My heart stopped.

"Believe me, I'm not happy about it. She called me to come fetch you," he continued with obvious reluctance. It was as if his mouth fought opening and closing to produce the words. He gazed around our small apartment. "What a pig sty! How does anyone live here?"

Before I could respond, he spun on me. "Get your things together. I don't want to stay here a moment longer than I have to."

"How long is she going to be in jail?" I asked, the tears beginning to burn under my eyelids.

"I don't know. Years, maybe," he said without emotion. "She was still on probation from that last thing. It's late. I have to get up in a few hours and go to work. Get a move on," he ordered.

"Why can't I just stay here?" I moaned.

"For the simple reason that the court won't permit it. I thought you were a smart kid. If you don't come with me, they'll put you in a foster home," he added.

For a long moment, I considered the option. I'd be better off with complete strangers than with him.

"And for another reason, I promised your

mother." He studied my face a moment and smiled coldly. "I know what you're thinking. I was surprised she gave a damn, too," he said.

My breath caught, and I couldn't swallow. I had to turn away so he wouldn't see the tears escaping and streaming down my cheeks. I hurried into the bedroom and opened the dresser drawers to take out my clothes. The only suitcase I had was small and had to be tied together with belts to close. I found it in the back of my closet and started to pack it.

Uncle Reuben stepped in and looked at the bedroom. "It stinks in here," he said.

I kept packing. I didn't know how long I would really live with him and Aunt Clara, but I didn't want to run out of socks and panties. "You don't need all that," he said when I reached into the closet for more clothes. "I don't want roaches in my house. Just take the basics."

"All I have is basics, some shirts and jeans and two dresses. And I don't have roaches in my clothes."

He grunted. I never liked Uncle Reuben. He was full of prejudice, often telling Mama that her problems began when she got herself involved with a Cuban. He liked to hold himself higher than us because he had been promoted and wore a suit to work.

I had two cousins, William, who was nine, and Jennifer, who was fourteen. William was a meek, quiet boy who, like me, enjoyed being by himself. He said very little, and once I heard Aunt Clara say the school thought he was nearly autistic. Jennifer was stuck-up. She had a way of holding her head back and talking down her nose that made everyone feel she thought she was superior. Once, when I was five, I got so frustrated with her I stomped on her foot and nearly broke one of her toes.

I finished packing and scooped up a pair of jeans and a sweater. Uncle Reuben stood there watching me as I walked past him to the bathroom to change. When I came out, he had my suitcase in his hand and was waiting in the doorway.

"Let's go," he urged. "I feel like I could catch some disease in here."

He, Aunt Clara, and my cousins lived in a nice A-frame two-story house. Mama and I didn't visit that often, but I was always envious of their yard, their nice furniture and clean bathrooms. William had his own room, and Jennifer had hers. The house was in a smaller village far enough away from the city so that I would have to go to a different school.

"Where am I going to stay?" I asked Uncle Reuben as I slipped on my sneakers.

"Clara's fixing up her sewing room for you. She has a pullout in it. Then we'll see," he said. "Come on."

"Should I just leave everything?" I asked, gazing about the apartment.

"What's there to leave? Old dishes, hand-me-down furniture, and rats? I wouldn't even bother locking the door," he muttered, and started down the stairs.

I paused in the doorway. He was right. It was a hole in the wall, drab and worn, even rotten in places and full of apologies, but it had been home for me. For so long, these walls were my little world. I always dreamed of leaving it, but now that I actually was, I couldn't help feeling afraid and sad.

"Raven!" Uncle Reuben shouted from the bottom of the stairway.

"Shut up out there!" someone cried. "People's trying to sleep."

I closed the door quickly and hurried down after him. We burst into the empty streets. It was still dark. The rest of the world was asleep. He threw my suitcase into the trunk of his car and got in quickly. I followed and gazed sleepily out the window at the apartment house. Only one of the three bulbs over the entryway worked. Shadows hid the chipped and faded paint and broken basement windows.

"It's lucky for you I live close enough to come and get you," he said, "or tonight you'd be on your way to some orphanage."

"I'm not an orphan," I shot back.

"No. You're worse," he said. "Orphans don't have mothers like yours."

"How can you talk about your sister like that?" I demanded. No matter how bad Mama was, I couldn't just sit there and listen to him tear her down.

"Easy," he said. "This isn't the first time I've had to come rescue her or bail her out, is it? This time, she's really gone and done it, though, and I say that's good. Let it come to an end. She's a lost cause." He turned to me. "And I'm warning you from the start," he fired, pointing his long, thick right forefinger into my face as he drove, "I don't want you corrupting my children, hear? The first time you bring disgrace into my home, that will be the last. I can assure you of that."

I curled up as far away from him as I could squeeze my body and closed my eyes. This is a nightmare, I thought, just a bad dream. In a moment, I'll wake up and be on the pullout in our living room. Maybe I'll hear Mama stumbling into the apartment. Suddenly, that didn't seem so bad.

We drove mostly in silence the rest of the way. Occasionally, Uncle Reuben muttered some obscenity or complained about being woken out of a deep sleep by his drunken, worthless sister.

"There oughta be a way to disown your relatives, to walk into a courtroom and declare yourself an independent soul so they can't come after you or ruin your life," he grumbled. I tried to ignore him, to go back to sleep.

I opened my eyes when we pulled into the driveway. The lights were on downstairs. He got out and opened the trunk, nearly ripping my suitcase apart when he took it out. I trailed behind him to the front door. Aunt Clara opened the door before we got there.

Aunt Clara was a mystery to me. No two people seemed more unalike than she and Uncle Reuben. She was small, fragile, dainty, and soft-spoken. Her face was usually full of sympathy and concern, and as far as I could ever tell, she never looked down on us or said bad things about us, no matter what Mama did. Mama liked her and, ironically, often told me she felt sorrier for her than she did for herself.

"It's a bigger burden living with my brother," she declared.

Aunt Clara had light brown hair that was always neatly styled about her ears. She wore little makeup, but her face was usually bright and cheery, especially because of the deep blue in her warm eyes and the soft smile on her small lips. She was only a few inches taller than I was, and when she stood next to Uncle Reuben, she looked as if she could be another one of his children.

She waited for us with her hands clasped and pressed between her small breasts.

"You poor dear," she said. "Come right in."

"Poor dear is right," Uncle Reuben said. "You should see that place. How could a grown woman want to live there and let her child live there?"

"Well, she's out of there now, Reuben."

"Yeah, right," he said. "I'm going back to bed. Some people have to work for a living," he muttered, and charged through the house and up the small stairway. The banister shook under his grip as he pulled himself up the stairs. He had dropped my suitcase in the middle of the floor.

"Would you like a cup of warm milk, Raven?" Aunt Clara asked.

"No, thank you," I said.

"You're tired, too, I imagine. This is all a bad business for everyone. Come with me. I have the sewing room all ready for you."

The sewing room was downstairs, just off the living room. It wasn't a big room, but it was sweet with flowery wallpaper, a light gray rug, a table with a sewing machine, a soft-backed wooden chair, and the pullout. There was one big window with white cotton curtains that faced the east side of the house, so the sunlight would light it up in the morning. On the walls were some needlework pictures in frames that Aunt Clara had done. They were scenes with farmhouses and animals and one with a woman and a young girl sitting by a brook.

"You know where the bathroom is, right down the hall," she said. "I wish we had another bedroom, but . . ."

"This is fine, Aunt Clara. I hate to take away your sewing room."

"Oh, it's nothing. I could do the same work someplace else. Don't you give it another thought, child. Tomorrow, you'll just rest, and maybe, before the day is out, we'll go over to the school and get you enrolled. We don't want you falling behind."

I hated to tell her how behind I already had fallen.

"Here's a new toothbrush," she said, indicating it on the desk. "I had one from the last time I went to the dentist."

"Thank you, Aunt Clara."

She gazed at me a moment and then shook her head and stroked my hair.

"The things we do to our children," she muttered, kissed me on the forehead, and left to go upstairs.

I stood there for a moment. To Aunt Clara, this room wasn't much, but to me, it was better than a luxury hotel. Her house smelled fresh and clean, and it was so quiet, no creaks, no voices coming through the walls, no footsteps pounding on the ceiling.

I got undressed and slipped under the fresh comforter. The pullout was firmer than ours, and the pillows were fluffy. I was so comfortable and so tired that I forgot for the moment that Mama was in jail. I was too tired, too frightened, and too confused to think anymore. I closed my eyes.

I opened them again when I felt someone was looking at me. It was morning. Sunlight poured through the window. I had forgotten where I was and sat up quickly. William was standing there gaping at me.

"Mama says you're going to live with us now," he said slowly.

I scrubbed my face with my palms and took a deep breath as it all came rushing back over me.

"William, get your rear end back in here

right now and finish your breakfast," I heard Uncle Reuben shout.

William hesitated and then hurried out. I lay back on my pillow and stared up at the ceiling.

"Your mother's in jail," I heard Jennifer say from the doorway.

I just turned and gazed at her. She had her light brown hair tied back with a ribbon. She was a tall girl with a large bone structure that made her look heavier than she was. Aunt Clara's features were overpowered by Uncle Reuben's, so that Jennifer's nose was wider and longer, as was her mouth. She had Aunt Clara's eyes, but they seemed out of place in so large a face. She was wide in the waist, too. Whenever I saw Uncle Reuben with her, however, he always treated her as if she were some raving beauty. There was never any question in my mind that he favored her over William. William was too small and fragile, too much like Aunt Clara.

"That's what your father says," I replied.

"Well, he wouldn't lie about it, would he? Jesus, what an embarrassment. And now you're going to be in my school, too," she complained.

"Well, I don't want to be," I said.

"Just don't tell anyone about your

mother. We'll make up some story," she decided.

"Like what?" I asked dubiously.

She stood there, staring in at me and thinking. "I know," she said with a smile. "We'll say she's dead."

2

Cinderella's Nightmare

"Who do you think you are, some princess?" Uncle Reuben bellowed from the doorway. "Everybody's up and havin' breakfast. Clara ain't gonna be waitin' on you."

"I was getting up," I said. "I didn't realize how late it was. There's no clock in this room, and I don't have a watch."

"No clock? I'll make sure I get you a clock. Those kind of excuses won't work here."

"It's not an excuse. It's the truth," I said.

He stood in the doorway with his hands on his hips. Then he glanced down the hall and stepped into the sewing room.

"We're going to set some rules down in concrete right now," he declared. "First, from now on, you're up before everybody. You set the table for breakfast, and you put on the coffee. Before you head off for school, make sure the table's cleared and the dishes and silverware are put away. When you come home from school, I expect you to help Clara around here. I want to see you cleaning the house, washing windows and floors. You'll help her with the laundry, too. This ain't a free ride just because your mother is a major screw-up, understand?"

I glared at him.

"When I ask you a question, I expect an answer. You need discipline. You're like some sort of wild animal livin' over there in that hole with that drunk of a sister of mine. That's all ended today, hear? Well?"

"I wasn't living like a wild animal," I shot back.

He smirked. "It looks like I'm going to end up bein' your legal guardian. That means you report to me, and I'm warning you right now, Raven, I don't spare the rod and spoil the child. Understand? Well?" He brought his large hand up. The palm looked as wide as a paddle.

"Yes," I said. "Yes."

He was practically standing over me, his face dark red with fury. I had no doubt he would strike me if he saw fit to do so, and I was afraid.

"Raven," he muttered with a twist in his lips. "What kind of a name is that to give a girl, anyway? She must have been drunk the day you was born."

"I like my name," I insisted. He was terrifying, but I had some pride.

He stood there a few minutes longer, gazing down at me. I pulled the comforter up to my shoulders, but I felt as if he could see right through it.

"I know you're growing older and growing fast, and I remember what happened to your mother, how she was when the boys started looking her way. You better not be taking the same road. I don't want you corrupting my Jennifer, hear?"

I turned away, the tears in my eyes making it impossible to look up at him anymore. I wasn't some disease. I wouldn't infect his precious Jennifer.

He grunted and left the room. I could hear him telling Aunt Clara what he had told me, what he wanted to be my chores. She didn't argue. A little while later, I heard him leave with Jennifer and William. I waited and rose.

"You hungry, dear?" Aunt Clara asked as I went to the bathroom.

"Just a little," I said.

"Coffee is still warm, and I have eggs if you want, even oatmeal."

"I'll take care of myself, Aunt Clara. Please don't think you have to wait on me," I said.

"Don't you worry about that," she said.

I got dressed and found myself some cold cereal. Aunt Clara poured me some orange juice and sat with me as I ate.

"Reuben's bark is worse than his bite," she said, trying to reassure me. "He's just upset with the surprise and all. Don't pay no mind to all those orders he gave."

"I don't mind helping out," I told her. "I did most of it at home, anyway."

"I bet you did." She nodded and sipped some coffee.

"Aunt Clara, what's going to happen to my mother? Is she really going to jail for a long time?" I asked.

"I don't know. Reuben mumbled something about them maybe putting her in a drug rehabilitation program, but we'll have to wait and see. You know, it's not her first time getting herself into big trouble," she added.

I nodded. There was no sense pretending it wasn't true or living in a dream world. Mama was in very big trouble, and that meant I was in trouble, too. Who wanted to live here with a cousin like Jennifer and an uncle like Uncle Reuben? I'd rather be in the streets.

"You just rest up a bit, honey," Aunt Clara said. "You've been through a terrible shock. After I tend to some chores, we'll have lunch, and right after that, I'll run you over to the school to get you enrolled, okay?"

"I'll help you with your chores, Aunt Clara. It's what Uncle Reuben wants, anyway," I said, "and it will help keep the peace."

"Ain't you the smart one?" she said, smiling. She tapped my hand. "Just sit here and finish your breakfast first."

She left and went upstairs. When I was done, I washed all the dishes and cleaned the table. I joined her just as she was starting on Jennifer's room. I paused in the doorway, shocked at the mess. Clothes were strewn about, and there was a dish with left-over apple pie on the floor by the bed, where the phone had been left as well. I imagined she had been sitting there talking to some friends and eating the pie, but why did she just leave it? Wasn't she worried about mice and bugs?

The bed was unmade, and the bathroom

38

she shared with William looked as if someone had had to leave in a hurry. Makeup was uncovered, the sink was still full of cloudy water, an open lipstick tube was on its side, the toothpaste was uncovered with some of it dripped onto the counter, a washcloth dangled on the doorknob, and there were magazines on the floor by the toilet. The shower door was open, a wet towel on the floor beside it.

Aunt Clara began to clean up without making a comment about the mess.

"Why does she leave her room and bathroom like this, Aunt Clara? Talk about living in a pig sty," I muttered. "I guess Uncle Reuben doesn't look in here often."

"Oh, he does," Aunt Clara said with a deep sigh. "And I've been after her, but Jennifer . . . Jennifer's a little spoiled," she admitted.

"A little? This looks like spoiled rotten," I said, but I pitched in and helped. I cleaned the bathroom until it looked spotless, even washing down the mirrors that were smudged with lipstick and makeup.

William's room was actually more organized and cleaner. The messiest thing was his unmade bed. After I straightened up his room, I went down and cleaned up the sewing room. I put the pullout back together so it didn't look like a bedroom. With my few things neatly put away, no one would even know I had slept there.

"You don't have to do that every day," Aunt Clara commented. "You can just close the door."

"I'm sure Uncle Reuben wouldn't like that," I told her.

She didn't argue. Even though he wasn't here, his shadow seemed to linger. The way Aunt Clara looked over her shoulder, it was almost as if she believed the shadow would tell him things we had said.

After we cleaned up the bedrooms, she began to vacuum the living room. I polished some furniture and swept the kitchen floor. I had to keep busy so I wouldn't think too much about Mama sitting in jail.

"You are a good worker, Raven. I hope some of your good habits will spill off onto my Jennifer," she said, but not with much optimism.

She prepared chicken salad for our lunch, and we sat and talked. I really didn't know much about her. She described where she had been brought up and how she had met Uncle Reuben. She said he had just started working with the public works department, and she had just graduated from high school.

40

"He was like an Atlas out there on the highway. With his shirt off and his muscles gleaming in the sunlight. He was a lot trimmer then," she recalled fondly. She laughed. "One day, he pretended to have road work right in front of my parents' house just so he could visit with me. We got married about four months later. My mother hoped I would at least go to a secretarial school, but you're impulsive when you're young," she remarked, and looked very thoughtful for a few moments. Then she shook her head and patted my hand. "Don't you go jumping into the arms of the first man you see, honey. Stand back, listen to your head instead of your heart, and take your time."

It seemed to me that every woman I ever met gave me the same advice. I was beginning to believe that love was a trap men set for unsuspecting women. They told us what we wanted to hear. They wrote promises in gold. They filled our heads with dreams and made it all seem easy, and then they satisfied themselves and went off to trap another innocent young woman. Even Aunt Clara, who had married her young sweetheart, discovered she had gotten caught in a trap. Uncle Reuben ruled his house like an ogre, turning her into a glorified maid instead of putting her up on a pedestal as I was sure he had promised. She just shook her head and threaded herself through her days like a rat caught in a maze.

After lunch, she drove me over to the school. It was smaller and seemed quieter than mine. The principal, Mr. Moore, a stout, thick-necked man of about forty, invited us into his office. He listened to Aunt Clara and then called his secretary and dictated orders quickly.

"I want you to contact her previous school, get the guidance counselor, get her records sent here ASAP, Martha," he said. I was impressed with his take-charge demeanor. "I suppose you know that we'll have to get some sort of instructions from Child Welfare as to her status. You and your husband are going to be her legal guardians, of course."

"Yes, of course," Aunt Clara said.

"She'll do fine," he concluded, gazing at me. "I know this isn't easy for you, but you should consider what it will be like for your new teachers. They have the added burden of bringing you up to par in their classes. The subjects might be the same, but everyone has his or her way of doing things, and there are bound to be differences. Some teachers move through the curriculum

42

faster than others."

"I know," I said.

He nodded, staring at me a moment with his eyes dark and concerned. Then he smiled.

"On the other hand, you have a cousin attending classes here. She should be of great help. Your daughter is a year older than Raven?" he asked Aunt Clara.

"Yes."

"Not a big difference. You'll have similar interests, I'm sure. She can help fill you in on our rules and regulations, too. Keep your nose clean, and we'll all get along, okay?"

I nodded.

Mr. Moore suggested I attend classes immediately. "No sense wasting any more time. She can still sit in on math and social studies. She'll get her books in those classes, at least," he said.

"What a good idea," Aunt Clara agreed.

A student office assistant brought me to math class and introduced me to Mr. Finnerman, who gave me a textbook and assigned me the last seat in the first row. Everyone looked at me, watching my every move. I recalled how interested I used to be when a new student arrived. I was sure they were all just as curious.

One girl, a black girl who introduced herself as Terri Johnson, showed me the way to social studies and introduced me to some other students along the way. She called me "the new girl." As we approached the social studies room, I saw Jennifer coming down the hall with two girlfriends at her side. The moment her eyes set on me, she stopped and moaned.

"That's her," I heard her tell them as she passed by without saying hello.

It was worse when social studies class ended and I had to find the right schoolbus home. Jennifer didn't wait for me, and when I found the bus, she was already seated in the rear with her friends, pretending she didn't know me. I sat up front and talked to a thin, dark-haired boy named Clarence Dunsen, who had a bad stutter. It made him shy but also very suspicious. When he did speak to me, he waited to see if I was going to ridicule him. I looked back at Jennifer, whose laugh resounded through the bus louder than anyone else's.

Please, Mama, I thought, be good, make promises, crawl on the floor if you have to, but get out and take me home, take me anywhere, just get me away from here.

"I got news," Aunt Clara said as soon as we entered the house.

"What?" I gasped, holding my new text-books tightly against me.

"Your mother's not going to jail."

"Thank God," I cried. I was going to add, "And good riddance to you, Jennifer Spoiled Head," but Aunt Clara wasn't smiling. She shook her head. "What else, Aunt Clara?"

"She has to be in drug rehabilitation. She could be there for some time, Raven. They won't even let her call you until her therapist says so."

"Oh," I said, sinking into a chair.

"It's better than it could have been," Aunt Clara said.

"Great. I have an aunt in drug rehabilitation," Jennifer whined. She turned her eyes on me like two little spotlights of hate. "You better do what I said and tell everyone your mother is dead," Jennifer warned.

I just looked at her.

"Don't talk like that, Jennifer," Aunt Clara said. "And you should know your cousin helped me clean your room. See if you can keep it that way."

"So what? She should clean our house. You heard what Daddy said. She's living off us, isn't she?" Jennifer fired back.

"Jennifer!" Aunt Clara cried. "Where's your charity and your love?"

"Love? I don't love her. It was hard enough to explain who she was. Everyone wanted to know why she's so dark. I had to tell them what her father was," she complained.

"Jennifer."

"You're not better than me because your skin's whiter," I charged.

"Of course, she isn't," Aunt Clara said. "Jennifer, I never taught you such terrible things."

"It's not fair, Mama. My friends are all wondering about our family now. It's not fair!" she moaned.

"Stop that talk, or I'll tell your father," Aunt Clara said.

"Tell him," she challenged, smirked, and walked up the stairs.

"I don't know where she gets that streak of meanness," Aunt Clara muttered.

I gazed up at her. Was she that blind or deliberately hiding her head in the sand? It was easy to see that Jennifer had inherited the meanness from Uncle Reuben.

"I'm sorry," Aunt Clara said.

"Don't worry about it, Aunt Clara. I'll be fine with or without Jennifer's friendship."

The door opened and closed, and William came sauntering in. He looked up at me with shy eyes.

"How was your day in school, William?" Aunt Clara asked.

He dug into his notebook and produced a spelling test on which he had received a ninety.

"That's wonderful! Look, Raven," she said, showing me.

"Very good, William. I'll have to come to you for help with my spelling homework."

He looked appreciative but took the test back quickly and shoved it into his notebook.

"Do you want some milk and cookies, William?" Aunt Clara asked him.

He shook his head, glanced at me with as close to a smile as he could manage, and then hurried up to his room.

"He's so shy. I never realized how shy. Doesn't he have any friends to play with after school?" I asked, watching him leave.

Aunt Clara shook her head sadly.

"He stays to himself too much, I know. The counselor at school called me in to discuss him. His teachers think he's too withdrawn. They all say he never raises his hand in class. He hardly speaks to the other students. You see him. He looks like a turtle about to crawl back in his shell. I don't know why," she added, her eyes filling with tears. I felt like putting my arm around her.

"He'll grow out of it," I said, but she didn't smile.

She shook her head. "Something's not right, but I don't know why. I took him to a doctor. He's healthy, hardly even gets a cold, but something . . ." Her voice trailed off. Then she turned to me with teary eyes and asked, "What makes a young boy behave like that?"

I didn't know then.

But I would soon learn why.

Only I wouldn't be able to find the words to tell her.

3

Fly Away Home

"Drug rehabilitation," Uncle Reuben muttered as he chewed his forkful of sirloin steak. Whenever Mama and I had steak, it was usually warmed-up leftovers she had brought back from Charlie's. "That's a waste of government money," he continued, chewing as he talked. He seemed to grind his teeth over the bitter words as well as his meat.

"It's not a waste of money if it helps her," Aunt Clara said softly.

He stopped chewing and glared at her.

"Helps her? Nothing can help her. She's a lost cause. Best thing they could do would be to lock her up and drop the key into the sewer."

Jennifer laughed. I looked up from my

plate and fixed my eyes on her.

"Stop staring at me," she complained. "It isn't polite to stare, is it, Daddy?"

Uncle Reuben glanced at me and then nodded. "No, it ain't, but how would she know?"

Jennifer laughed again and smiled at me. My meat tasted like chunks of cardboard and stuck in my throat. I stopped eating and sat back. "I'd like to be excused," I said.

"Like hell you will, until you finish that," Uncle Reuben said, nodding at my plate. "We don't waste food here."

Jennifer cut into her steak and chomped down with a wide smile on her chubby face, pretending to savor every morsel. "It's delicious," she said.

"It's not polite to talk with food in your mouth," I said quickly.

William looked up with a gleeful smile in his eyes. Jennifer stopped chewing and swung her eyes at Uncle Reuben. He continued to scoop up his potatoes, shoveling the food into his mouth as if he had to finish in record time.

"I have a homemade pecan pie, Reuben. Your favorite," Aunt Clara said.

He nodded as if he expected no less. They're all spoiled, I thought.

"I got an eighty on my English test

today," Jennifer told him.

"No kidding? Eighty. That's good," Uncle Reuben said.

"I have a chance to make the honor roll if Mr. Finnerman gives me a decent grade in math this quarter," she bragged.

"Wow. Hear that, Clara? That's my little girl making her daddy proud."

"Yes. That's very good," Aunt Clara said. "William came home with a ninety in spelling," she added.

William looked at Uncle Reuben, but he just continued chewing with only the slightest nod. "I guess I gotta go get the paperwork done on her," he said finally. "Everything go all right with the school?"

"Yes," Aunt Clara said. "She's enrolled."

"What kind of grades you been getting?" he asked me.

"I pass everything," I said, looking away quickly.

"I bet," he said. "Your mother ever ask you how you were doing in school?"

"Yes, she has," I said with indignation. He curled his lips. "She had to sign my report card, so she saw my grades all the time."

"You never forged her signature?" Jennifer asked with a smile that could freeze lava.

51

"Why? Is that what you do?" I fired back.

"Hardly. I don't have to do that. I pass for real," she said. "Daddy signs my report cards, don't you, Daddy?"

"Every time," he agreed. He pushed back from the table and stood. "If she's going to waste food, Clara, you see you don't give her as much to start. I work hard for my money to pay for everything," he added, directing himself to me.

Even though my stomach was protesting, I forced myself to swallow the last piece of meat and another forkful of green beans.

"I want to catch the news. Call me when coffee and pie is ready," he added, and left the kitchen to go watch television.

My eyes followed him out, and then I looked at William, who was staring at me sympathetically. I smiled at him, and his face brightened.

"I gotta go do my homework, Ma. I don't have to do anything with the dinner dishes anyway, right? You got her," Jennifer said, nodding at me.

"You should still help out, Jennifer."

"I can't. You heard Daddy. He wants me to make the honor roll. Don't you want me to finish my homework?" she whined.

"Of course."

"Okay, then," she said, jumping up. "I'll

come down later for a piece of pie."

She left the kitchen. Aunt Clara shook her head sadly.

"I'll help," William said. He started to clear the table with me.

"You want to see the birdhouse I built?" he asked me when we were finished.

Aunt Clara smiled at me, happy William was emerging a little from his shell.

"Sure," I said.

"It's up in my room. I made it myself," he said. I followed him up to his room, and he took it off the shelf. It was a triangular-shaped house with dried corncobs attached to the outside.

"I glued all those on," he said, showing me how secure the cobs were.

I handled it gently. "This is wonderful, William. It must have been hard to build this from scratch. How long did it take?"

"A couple of days," he said proudly. "As soon as I save up enough, I'm going to buy some binoculars so I can see the birds that come to my house up close. Do you know anything about birds?"

I shook my head, and he went to his desk to get an encyclopedia of birds. It contained brightly colored photos of birds, their habitats, and the type of food they ate. He then showed me another book that had instructions on building birdhouses.

"That's the next one I want to build." He pointed to a double-decker birdhouse.

"That's beautiful. You can build that?"

"Sure," he said confidently. "I'll let you know when I get the materials, and you could watch if you want."

"Thanks," I said.

He gave me his best smile, one that truly brightened his eyes.

"I better start on my homework," I told him.

I left, and as I passed Jennifer's door, which was partly open, I saw her curled on the floor, talking on her phone. I paused, and she looked up at me.

"What are you doing, spying on me?" she snapped.

"Hardly," I said. "But I thought you had to do your homework, or are you taking a course in gossip?" I continued down the stairs, my heart pounding. I heard her slam her door closed behind me.

Since the sewing room was so close to the dining room, I could hear Uncle Reuben's conversation with Aunt Clara while he had his coffee and pie.

"We're not going to go and spend a lot of money on new clothes for her. I want to see if we can get some sort of government help.

I think if you take in a kid, they give you some support money."

"She needs things, Reuben," Aunt Clara said softly. "Shouldn't you go back and see what else she has in the apartment?"

"What good would that do? We'd only have to have it deloused."

"You can't just let her wear what she has," Aunt Clara insisted softly.

"Okay, okay, get her a couple of things. But I don't want you spending a lot of money, Clara. We got Jennifer, who needs new things. You see how fast she's growing."

"Maybe Jennifer will share some of her things with Raven," Aunt Clara said.

He grunted and then added, "If she does, you make sure Raven is clean before she puts anything of Jennifer's on."

"Oh, she's clean, Reuben. She's really a very nice young lady, despite her life with your sister."

"We'll see," he said. I heard him rise. "Make sure she cleans all this up before she goes to sleep. I want her to appreciate what she gets here."

"She does."

He didn't respond. I heard him go back into the living room and turn up the television. Then I went to help Aunt Clara.

"You don't have to do this, Raven," she whispered. "There's not much left. Go do your homework."

"I didn't have that much, Aunt Clara. I have to meet with my teachers for a while after school each day for the next week to catch up. When will we know when Mama can talk to me?" I asked.

She shook her head. "I don't know, honey. Reuben will find out more tomorrow."

"He should have made more over William's spelling test," I mumbled. "And an eighty isn't such a great grade."

She looked at me with not so much fear in her eyes as cautious agreement. "I know," she said. "I've been after him to spend more time with William."

"I'm not so sure that would help," I muttered, mostly to myself. If she heard, she didn't respond. Then she paused and looked as if she saw a ghost. I turned.

Uncle Reuben was standing in the doorway.

"She should do that herself, Clara. You need to come in and rest," he ordered, his eyes burning through me.

"There's nothing left to do, Reuben."

He continued to stare. Had he heard me?

"All right, Reuben. I'm coming," she

said. She wiped her hands on a dish towel and left the kitchen. He let her pass, glanced at me again, and then followed her.

From what I had seen already, I realized Uncle Reuben whipped his family around this house with a look, a word, a gesture. He was the puppet master, and they jumped when he tugged at their strings. I felt as if he was tying strings around my arms and legs, too, and soon I would be just another puppet.

After finishing my homework, I made my bed and changed into the one nightgown I owned. Lying there and staring out through my one window at the stars that popped in between passing clouds, I thought that somehow I had been turned into Cinderella without the magic slipper or fairy godmother. There would be no magic in my life.

Once, I spent my time dreaming about far-off places, beautiful houses, handsome young men, gala dances, beautiful clothes and jewels. I was in my own movie, spinning out the scenes on the walls of my imagination. It took me out of the small apartment.

I had to laugh.

Here I was, out, with a family, going to a new school, and what did I dream of?

Getting back to my small apartment.

I actually grew to like the new school. Because my classes were much smaller, the teachers took more time with me, and I also began to make some friends. Jennifer continued to avoid me as much as possible, but I began to accept it. From what I saw of the friends she had, girls who were mostly like her, selfish, vain, and sneaky, I more than accepted it. I welcomed it. There were much nicer kids to know.

Jennifer was far from the goody-goody she pretended to be in front of Uncle Reuben, too. She was right in there with the girls who smoked in the girls' room, and from what I was told and what I saw, she often cheated on her homework and tests. I could see that her teachers weren't very fond of her, either. Terri Johnson told me she knew for a fact that Jennifer and her friends went on shoplifting sprees at the mall just for the thrill of it. Here she was, a girl with parents, a nice home, and all, and she wasn't any better than the girls I had known who came from broken families and who lived in much more unpleasant places. I wondered what Uncle Reuben would do if he found out any of this about his precious perfect daughter.

One day in the cafeteria, Jennifer paused with two of her friends at my table. I stopped talking and looked up at her.

"You've fallen behind on the laundry," she said. "I need that blue and white blouse tomorrow. See that it's done."

My mouth fell open as I looked from her to the smirking faces of her friends.

"Why don't you wash it yourself, then?" I shot back.

"You're supposed to be earning your room and board, aren't you?"

"What about you?" I countered.

"I don't have to. I have parents," she replied smugly. "Just get it done, or I'll tell Daddy," she threatened, and walked off laughing.

Terri looked down, embarrassed for me.

"She's a spoiled brat," I said. I wanted to say a lot more, but it was hard to talk. My words got choked in my throat because it was tight from fighting back my tears.

"I'd rather live with a snake than that," Terri offered, and the girls at my table all laughed.

"Yeah, well, that's what I'm doing," I muttered, "living with a snake."

When I got home from school that day, I found her precious blue and white blouse in the hamper. Before I put it into the washing machine, I poked a hole in the shoulder of the blouse with the pointed end of my math compass. After dinner on Tuesdays, Aunt Clara and I folded and ironed clothes. She didn't notice the hole in the blouse, and she brought everything up to Jennifer's room. It wasn't until the next morning, when I was sure she was going to wear it just to show off at school, that we heard her scream.

I had already risen and gotten dressed. Aunt Clara was with me in the kitchen preparing breakfast.

"What in the world . . ." She hurried to the foot of the stairway.

Jennifer was on the landing in her skirt and bra, holding up the blouse.

"Just look at this, Ma. Just look."

"What the hell is it?" Uncle Reuben demanded, coming from his bedroom and buttoning his shirt.

"There's a hole in my favorite blouse, and she did it. She did, Daddy!"

She showed him the blouse. He looked at it and then down the stairs at me.

"Did you do this?"

I shook my head. "I didn't even see it, or I would have told Aunt Clara," I said.

"Why would Raven do such a thing?" Aunt Clara asked.

"Because she's jealous," Jennifer cried.

"I don't even like that blouse. It's too old-fashioned, like something a grandmother might wear," I said dryly.

"It is not! Everyone's wearing these blouses. You don't know anything about style!"

"Please, Jennifer," Aunt Clara said, "stop yelling."

William came out and looked at everyone, his face full of surprise. I smiled at him, and he smiled back.

"If I knew you put a hole in this . . ." Uncle Reuben threatened. He looked at the blouse again. "I don't know how this kind of a hole would get in there."

"Bugs can do that," I said. He looked up sharply.

"We don't have bugs, or at least we didn't before you came," he said. "Clara?"

"Oh, I'll just buy her a new one today, Reuben."

"I'd better not see anything else like this," he warned. He gave Jennifer the blouse back and returned to his bedroom to finish dressing. Aunt Clara went back to the kitchen, and Jennifer and I looked at each other.

"You'll be sorry," she said. "I'm going to wear it anyway and let everyone know what you did."

"Suit yourself," I said. "You'll only make

a bigger fool of yourself."

I winked at William.

"What are you laughing at?" she snapped at him, and ran back into her room.

For the first time in a long time, I had a great appetite and ate a big breakfast. Even Uncle Reuben was impressed at how I didn't leave a crumb.

4

A Close Call

When we boarded the schoolbus on Thursday, I had my arms full. Jennifer had to do a social studies project, and she had chosen to make a large visual chart, but there was a good reason she had made that choice. One of her girlfriends, Paula Gordon, who was talented in art, came over and really did most of it. Jennifer pretended she had done it all, and when she showed it to Uncle Reuben on Thursday morning, he raved about it as if it were something a famous artist like Rembrandt or that artist who cut off his ear for his girlfriend might have done. I thought any one of the birdhouses William made in his wood shop all by himself was twice the accomplishment, and yet I never once heard Uncle Reuben even mention them, much less praise him about them.

As usual, Jennifer basked in the compliments her father tossed like wedding rice over her. When we got ready to leave the house, she was very concerned about getting her precious project to school undamaged. She surprised me by pausing at the door, and in the sweetest voice she could manage, she asked me to do her a favor. I saw she had made sure to ask in front of Uncle Reuben.

"You know how rough the kids are on the bus, Raven. I have to protect my chart. Can you please carry my books, my notebooks, and my lunch bag for me? Please. Someday, I'll do you a favor," she promised, flicking her eyelashes at Uncle Reuben.

What else could I do but agree? I felt like some slave walking behind her, my arms laden with my books and my lunch bag as well as hers. She paraded down the sidewalk and onto the bus, holding her chart up high enough for everyone to see.

"Someone make a place for Raven. She's carrying my things for me," she announced.

It wasn't necessary. I always sat with Clarence Dunsen. She just wanted everyone to know that she could get me to do things for her.

When we arrived at school, she surprised me by taking only the books and notebooks she needed for her morning classes.

"Bring everything else to lunch. I've got to carry this around until social studies," she said in front of her friends, who stood there with thin smiles and laughing eyes.

"Why don't you just bring it to social studies now?" I asked her.

"And take a chance that someone might sabotage it? Never. Remember what happened to Robert Longo's ant farm in science class?" she asked her entourage. They all nodded. "Someone poured water in it and drowned all the ants."

"I wonder who would do that," I said dryly.

"Thanks, Raven," she said, taking her morning class books and shooting off before I could refuse.

I lugged her things along with mine to my first class.

"How come you have two lunches today?" Terri Johnson asked me in English class. I told her, and she raised her eyebrows sharply, the skin in her forehead forming small furrows.

"She's just trying to show off," I said, but Terri still looked suspicious.

"She could ask one of her slaves to do that. Those girls would be glad to do her favors. I've seen it. I don't know what she's up to, but as my granny tells me all the time, a snake can't be a rabbit," she added.

I laughed, but later I began to think a little more about it, too. Just before class ended, I looked at what I thought was Jennifer's lunch bag, only I noticed my name was on it. Why would that be? I wondered.

I opened what was supposed to be Jennifer's lunch bag. We usually had the same thing. I knew because I had helped Aunt Clara make the lunches. There was an extra small pack wrapped in wax paper in hers. I glanced up to be sure Mrs. Broadhurst wasn't looking my way, and then I unwrapped the wax paper.

A cold but electric chill shot through my heart. I had seen this before. I knew what a joint was. I had seen and smelled pot around my old apartment. Lila Thomas had tried to get me to smoke it with her once.

I looked over at Terri. She saw immediately from the expression on my face that something was wrong. I lowered my hand to the side, looked at the teacher, and then opened my hand. When I looked back at Terri, she was nodding with satisfaction. Five minutes before class ended, the real reason Jennifer wanted me to carry her lunch was clearly revealed.

"Excuse me, Mrs. Broadhurst," the student office volunteer said from our doorway. "Mr. Moore would like to see Raven Flores immediately. He wants her to bring all her things, too," she added.

"Raven," she said, nodding at me. I glanced at Terri, whose eyes were filled with worry. I smiled and winked at her to reassure her.

I scooped everything into my arms, glanced once more at Terri, and followed the student volunteer. As I left the classroom, I stuffed the wax paper and joint into my bra. I had seen girls do this at my old school. No one would look there. It was a very serious thing to strip-search a student. Male teachers were terrified of even suggesting such a thing, and the girls knew it.

Mr. Moore was standing at his desk when I entered his office. He gazed at me and then nodded at the student volunteer.

"Close the door," he told her. She glanced at me with interest, stepped out, and did so. "Sit," he ordered, nodding at the chair. I sat quickly, and he stood over me.

"It has always been my policy to handle my problems in house, if possible," he began, gazing at me quickly to catch my reaction. "That doesn't mean I don't tell parents what goes on. I have an obligation to do that, but the rest of the world doesn't have to see our dirty laundry."

"What do you want from me?" I demanded.

His eyebrows hoisted with surprise at my courage. "I know you've had a poor background and upbringing, and that goes to explain poor behavior, but you're at an age now when you will be held accountable for your actions, young lady. I can assure you of that."

I looked away, my eyes fixed on one of his plaques, and waited.

"If there is something illegal in your lunch bag, I want you to take it out now, leave it on my desk, and go to class. Later, we'll discuss it, and believe me, that is a major favor I'll be doing for you."

My heart thumped, and then I smiled. I leaned down and opened my lunch bag, slowly taking out the sandwich and the cookie. Then I turned the bag inside out and placed it next to the food. I waited.

"What about that bag?" he asked, nodding at the other.

"That's my cousin's, even though my name is somehow on it. I was doing her a favor. Her arms were full of books and her social studies project."

"How do I know that's hers if your name

is on it?" he asked.

"You don't, but we have the same lunch, so it doesn't matter," I said, and took out the sandwich and the cookie. I did the same thing with her bag, turning it inside out, and waited.

His eyes went from the harmless contents to my books and then to me.

"Can I at least know what you're looking for?" I asked.

"Never mind," he said. "Put all that back."

I did so slowly. "I don't think it's fair for me to be singled out for no reason," I said. "It's embarrassing to be called out of class like this."

His shoulders shot up as if I had snapped a rubber band in his face. "I have a very big responsibility here," he said. "Many young lives are in my hands, and" — he lifted a thick folder — "I have read your records from your previous school. Frankly, if you did all this here, I would consider having you taken to family court. I'm not surprised your mother's in prison."

"I haven't done anything wrong," I shot back at him.

"We'll see," he said.

"Who told you I did?" I asked.

"That's none of your concern. Very well,

return to your classes," he ordered. "And just remember," he said, tapping my previous school record folder, "I'll be keeping my eye on you."

I got up quickly and left his office. The bell had rung, so the secretary had to give me a late pass. When I got to my next class, Terri looked up expectantly. I nodded and smiled to let her know everything was fine. After class, I told her what I had done and what had happened.

"She tried to set me up and get me into trouble."

"It doesn't surprise me. Jennifer and her friends are always getting other people in trouble," Terri said. "You better watch your back."

"I will, but she'll find out she should watch hers, too," I said.

At lunch, Jennifer and her friends walked over to my table.

"I'll take my lunch," she said.

"I don't know which one is yours," I said. "Somehow, my name is on both bags. Luckily, we both have the same thing." I handed it to her. She looked at the girls and then at me.

"I heard you were called to the principal's office," she said. "Why did he want to see you?" She smiled at the girls. "I hope you didn't embarrass my parents."

"No, it was fine," I said, taking a sip from the straw in my milk container. "He just wanted to know what we were having for lunch. He said he heard we had the best homemade lunches," I added, and bit into my sandwich.

Even her friends had to laugh. She fumed, her face so crimson I thought the blood would shoot out of the top of her head like a geyser, and then she pivoted on her heels and marched away. Terri and the girls at my table laughed so hard that others in the cafeteria stopped talking to look our way.

"I guess there's a little snake in you, too," Terri said.

"What else? She and I are cousins, aren't we?" I said, and that made everyone laugh again.

But I wasn't finished, not yet, not quite.

On Saturday, Jennifer went off with her friends right after breakfast as she usually did on Saturdays. Aunt Clara tried to get her to take me along, but she resisted and complained.

"She doesn't have the same friends I do," she moaned.

"What does that mean?" Uncle Reuben asked quickly, fixing his eyes on me sharply. "Who are her friends?"

Jennifer shrugged. "She hangs out with black people. I suppose because she's so dark."

"No," I said. "I hang out with people of color who happen to be nice and not phony."

"Oh, and that's supposed to mean my friends are?"

I shrugged. "Because I'm new in the school, everyone is warning me about them," I said as nonchalantly as I could.

Her face looked as if she was facing a wall of fire. Before she could stutter out a response, Aunt Clara spoke. "You two should get along," she said. "You're just about the same age."

"I don't want Jennifer hanging out with any troublemakers," Uncle Reuben said.

"I don't hang out with troublemakers," I insisted. "It's just the opposite."

"Why can't she go with Jennifer and be with young people, too?" Aunt Clara asked softly.

"It's all right. I'm fine," I said.

I don't know why Aunt Clara suggested I go along anyway. She knew that Uncle Reuben would be home and would be watching to make sure I did my chores. Jennifer wouldn't lift a finger, and she certainly wouldn't have wanted to wait for me.

Shortly after Jennifer left, Aunt Clara and I began our weekly cleaning of the house. William wanted to help with the vacuuming, but Uncle Reuben chastised him.

"That's woman's work," he growled. "Let them do it. Why don't you go play baseball or football instead of spending all your time in your room?" he complained, which only sent William back to his room.

I gazed at Aunt Clara to see if she would speak up for William, but she looked away quickly and continued to clean. We went upstairs to start on the bedrooms, and I began as usual with Jennifer's mess. It was worse than ever, now that she knew I had to do most of the cleaning. Aunt Clara felt sorry for me and joined me in Jennifer's room. She started with making the bed. When she lifted the pillow, she stopped and stared down. I kept picking up clothes that had been flung about with apparent glee. A blouse actually dangled off the top of the vanity mirror.

"What's that?" Aunt Clara asked.

"What?"

I turned and watched her put the pillow down and then pluck the joint between her fingers. She smelled it and looked at me. I approached and leaned over to smell it, too.

Then I looked at her, my eyes wide, my head shaking slowly.

"Is this what I think it is?" she asked.

"Yes," I said. "I'm afraid so, Aunt Clara."

"Oh, dear. Oh, dear me. Oh, no. I'll have to tell Reuben." She hurried out of the room and down the stairs. Moments later, I heard Uncle Reuben come charging up, his footsteps so hard on the steps the whole house shook.

"What's going on here?" he demanded.

I stepped out of the bathroom, my arms full of wet towels for the laundry.

"I don't know," I said.

"Who put this there?" he demanded. Aunt Clara came up behind him. I stared at him.

"I really don't know, Uncle Reuben," I said.

"You didn't do it?"

"She was working on picking things up when I found it, Reuben. She didn't put it there," Aunt Clara said, and started to cry.

"And I suppose you don't know nothing about it?" Uncle Reuben followed.

I shook my head.

Uncle Reuben's eyes grew small and then widened. He gazed at Aunt Clara and then at me.

"We'll see about this when she gets

home," he fired. He shot another angry look in my direction and then left the room.

"Oh, dear," Aunt Clara said. "Oh, dear, dear." She followed after him.

I set down the towels, looked at Jennifer's picture on her dresser, the one in which she had the most conceited grin on her face, and smiled myself.

Jennifer's reaction was predictable. As soon as she was confronted with the evidence, she burst into tears and pointed her right forefinger at me like a pistol.

"She did it. She did it to get me into trouble," she accused.

Uncle Reuben nodded. "I've been thinking so," he said.

"How could I do it? I wasn't in your room until I went upstairs with Aunt Clara to clean the mess," I said quietly.

"You must have done it before."

"Why?"

"To get me in trouble," she whined.

"Why would I do that?" I asked. "Why would I stoop so low as to put something like that under your pillow?"

She stared at me hatefully. Then she turned to Uncle Reuben. "Daddy!" she moaned.

"Jennifer's never done anything like this

before," he said. "I'd bet you have."

"You'd lose," I said.

"Daddy, I didn't do it," Jennifer cried, stamping her foot.

"All right. All right. I believe you." He thought a moment. I could see there was an inkling of doubt in his mind. "We'll let it go for now, but I'll be on the lookout for any more trouble, even the slightest. If I find drugs in this house again, I'll bring the owner to the police. That's a promise," he said, directing his words mostly at me.

Jennifer looked satisfied and glanced at me with an expression of contentment. "I'm tired," she said. "I have to rest before I go to the movies."

She hurried away. Nothing more was said about it, but when we left for school the next day, she hurried up to me before mounting the steps to the bus.

"I know you did that with the joint."

"It was yours. You accidentally left it in your lunch bag, but I got it out in time so you wouldn't get in trouble. I thought you would appreciate my hiding it for you," I said, pretending to be dumb.

She stared at me, and then her eyes filled with cold understanding before she stepped onto the bus. Later, I told Terri, and the two of us had fun telling our other friends.

Jennifer avoided me most of the day. It was one of my best days at the new school, but I was still wishing it would all come to an end. I had had enough of Uncle Reuben and battling with Jennifer.

My hopes died a quick death when we got home that afternoon. Jennifer refused to talk to me on the bus and walked slowly so I would get to the house first. As soon as I entered, Aunt Clara stepped out of the living room, her hand clutching a handkerchief to her mouth.

"What's wrong?" I asked. Jennifer came up behind me.

"Your mother," Aunt Clara said. "She's gone and run off from the rehabilitation clinic. She's a fugitive."

"Great," Jennifer said. "Maybe she'll come for you, and you can run off together."

"Stop that talk!" Aunt Clara cried in a voice so sharp and shrill even I took note. "I won't have it."

Jennifer's eyes filled with tears. "You care more about her than you do me," she accused. Aunt Clara started to shake her head. "Yes, you do. But I'm not surprised," she added, and flew up the stairs.

"I should leave," I murmured, looking after her.

"Where would you go? You have to be with family," Aunt Clara insisted.

Family, I thought. That's a word I'll never understand.

5

Behind Closed Doors

"Can you believe it?" Uncle Reuben cried as he entered the house. "The police came to my office, came to see me at work! The police! Everyone sees them and wants to know what's going on. My sister, I had to tell them, has run away from her drug rehabilitation center, violated court orders. She's some kind of fugitive, and the police came to see if she's contacted me. I can tell you this. If she does have the nerve to contact me, I'll turn her in. She's dragging us all down with her!"

I was in my room trembling, but I could hear him slamming things around in the kitchen.

"Please don't get yourself so upset, Reuben," Aunt Clara pleaded.

"Don't get upset?" He laughed madly. "My sister's rotten through and through, Clara. She's like some dark, rancid piece of fruit stinking up the place. Now I got her juvenile delinquent to raise. Why didn't she think before she got herself pregnant by that no-good Cuban bum? The state's going to pay us for this. I'll see to that. I see this kind of thing all the time . . . women who can't afford to have children, who should never have children, just raining them down on the rest of us. That's why taxes is so high, you know, because of people like my sister and what she produces."

"You've got to stop this, Reuben. You'll get yourself sick," Aunt Clara said.

"Sick? I am sick, sick of it all." He groaned so loud I thought he was coming through the wall. "It's not like I didn't try to help my sister. I told her how a real man acts . . . I showed her. I showed her, all right."

"Reuben . . . I don't think you should get so worked up," Aunt Clara said. I could tell by the sound of her voice that she was nervous and wanted to change the subject.

What was Uncle Reuben saying about my mother? What had he showed Mama?

I heard him get up and walk to the stairway, pausing at my door. My heart thumped. I thought he would come bursting through the door and yell at me about my mother and how I was a drain on society. I kept my eyes to the floor and waited, holding my breath. A moment later, I heard him start up the stairs.

My eyes were burning with hot tears. I stared out the window.

Mama, how could you do this to me? Why did you run away? For a moment, I wondered if she would come here to get me, take me away from all this. I'd even hide out with her. Who was I fooling? I thought. I was probably the last thing she thought about when she fled. By now, she must be with one of her degenerate boyfriends, either hiding out or racing off to live in some hovel.

My mother seemed to be two different people to me now. Once, when I was younger, I thought of her as someone to love and someone who loved me, but somehow, somewhere, that all disappeared, and we started to live like two strangers. Maybe Uncle Reuben was right. Maybe my mother was just no good. Something had gone wrong inside her, and she could never be rehabilitated. She would never change.

Was that same bad germ inside me, too? Would I become like her someday, despite myself? Was Uncle Reuben right about that, too? I was my mother's daughter. I inherited something from her, and maybe that something was evil. I wasn't any sort of student. I had no real friends. I was afraid to have any ambitions, and so, when I tried to envision myself ten years from now, all I could see was the same lonely, lost person.

Uncle Reuben wasn't wrong. I was going to be just like my mother.

I sighed so deeply my chest ached. Then I stood up, wiped my eyes, and went to help Aunt Clara prepare dinner. She looked very tired and very sad herself. The way she held her shoulders slumped, kept her eyes down, and moved with tiny, insecure steps made her look even smaller than she was. It was as if she had shrunk inches since Uncle Reuben had come home. She was the one who looked pitiful, and yet she turned to me with sympathy flooding her eyes and shook her head.

"You poor dear," she said. "I know how you must feel. I'm sorry your mother has done these things. She should think what she's doing to you."

I didn't reply. I set the table, moving mechanically about the kitchen. I dreaded sitting at the dinner table with Uncle Reuben tonight. My throat was closing as it was. As soon as he began his tirade against my mother and complained about me, I would surely choke on anything that was in my mouth, and he would scream about my wasting the food he worked so hard to provide.

Suddenly, I felt dizzy and had to seize the top of a chair to keep myself from falling. Aunt Clara came running to me.

"What's wrong, Raven?"

"I don't know. My head just started to spin."

"You look white as a candle. Here, let me get you some cold water. Sit," she ordered, and I did so. My stomach churned. When she brought me the water, I held the glass with both hands and sipped. It did make me feel a little better.

"I want you to go lay down, honey," she said. "I don't need you to do anything. Go on. Rest. You've had a big shock."

She helped me to my feet and guided me back to the sewing room. I hadn't pulled out the bed yet, so she did it for me, and then I lay down.

"I still feel a little sick," I said.

"Oh, dear. If you're not better in a little while, I'll take you to the emergency room."

"No, I'm not that sick, Aunt Clara. I'll be all right," I promised.

She stroked my hair and felt my forehead.

"You don't feel too hot, but you're very clammy. It's all emotional, I'm sure," she said. "Just rest."

She brought the glass of water in and set it beside me. I settled under the blankets and felt a little better, but still my stomach flopped. I closed my eyes again, and before I knew it, I fell asleep, only to wake to the sound of Uncle Reuben's loud voice rumbling through the house like thunder demanding where I was and why I wasn't helping to serve the meal. I started to get up, and the room spun on me, so I had to lie back.

Their voices became indistinct mumbles, and I must have fallen asleep again, because when I opened my eyes this time, Aunt Clara was standing beside the bed with a tray in her hands.

"How are you feeling now, dear?" she asked.

I blinked, rubbed my face, and sat up slowly. Fortunately, the room didn't spin.

"Better."

"Good," she said. "Here, I brought you some dinner. You have to put something warm in your stomach."

"I'm not very hungry."

"I know, but it's best to eat when you're under such a strain. Go on," she said, placing the tray in my lap, "eat what you can."

"Jesus, serving her like she's some kind of special guest," I heard Uncle Reuben spit from the doorway.

"I told you she wasn't feeling well, Reuben. I want her to get some food down."

"Of course, she's not feeling well. Who would if they were brought up the way she was? It's a wonder she's not seriously sick with some bad disease," he concluded. "We might all come down with it, and you asking Jennifer to share clothes and such with her."

"I'm just as healthy as Jennifer," I fired back at him.

He smirked. "I can just imagine what your teeth are like. When were you to a dentist last?"

I hadn't been for nearly a year, so I didn't answer.

"See what I mean?" he said to Aunt Clara. "Either we get the state to help us, or . . ."

"Or what?" I shot back at him.

"Don't you be smart with me," he said, pointing his finger at me.

"Let her eat, Reuben. There's time to talk about all this," Aunt Clara pleaded softly.

He glared at her, and she looked down quickly. "Time? Yeah, there's time," he said sarcastically. "Lots of time. My sister ain't coming back for her. That's for sure," he added, and walked away.

I started to sob, my shoulders shaking so hard I thought my heart would split in two.

Aunt Clara put the tray down and sat beside me, embracing me. "Don't cry, dear. He doesn't mean what he says. He's upset because he was embarrassed at work. Please, you'll only make yourself sicker, and then what?"

I sucked in my breath and pulled back my tears.

"Please, eat something, Raven," Aunt Clara begged.

"All right," I said. "Thank you, Aunt Clara."

I started to eat, and she left. Afterward, William came to my door.

"I'll take your tray to the kitchen for you," he volunteered.

"Thank you," I said, smiling, "but I can do it, William. It's nice of you to offer, though."

He continued to stare at me.

"Is there something wrong?" I asked him.

"Are you feeling better now?"

"Yes, I am," I said. "Your mother was right. Hot food helped."

He smiled. "Good, because I want to show you the double-decker birdhouse. It's done," he declared.

"It is? Okay," I said.

I took my tray to the kitchen. Aunt Clara, who was watching television, came rushing in. "I'll do that, Raven."

"I'm fine now," I told her, and smiled.

"And you ate, too. Good," she said. She put my dishes in the dishwasher. "You just go and do your homework, or come watch television if you like, Raven."

"I'm going up to see William's new birdhouse, and then I'll do my homework," I explained.

"Oh. That's very nice," she said.

William looked proud. "Come on," he said, and I followed him up the stairs to his room.

As I sat and listened to him explain what kind of birds would feed in his house, I felt sorry for him, sorry that his father took so little interest in what he had accomplished. He was like a flower, stunted and pale because it received so little sunlight. He almost talked as much about his father making fun of his hobby as he did about why he loved making the houses. When I showed sincere interest in him and what he was doing, he wasn't sad or shy anymore. He practically beamed with pride.

"Thank you for showing me your work, William. I bet you could sell these birdhouses. They're so perfect," I told him, gazing around at his collection. It was impressive when I realized he had done all of it himself.

He beamed and strutted about his room, showing me his books on birds, his tools and paints, and some of his other creations.

"Do you have a favorite bird?" he asked me. "Because if you do, I'll make a special house for you."

"No. I don't really know very much about birds. We didn't have many trees around the apartment building."

"Oh, I guess not," he said. "I've been hoping to build a house for every kind of bird we get around here. But it takes money to buy all the wood and stuff. And every time I talk to Daddy about my projects, he just makes fun of me." He hung his head sadly.

"I wish I had some money to help you buy supplies," I told him.

"Don't worry. I'll get the money." He thought a moment and then decided to tell me how. "Daddy drops a lot of change behind the cushions on the sofa downstairs when he sprawls out to watch television. When nobody's around, I pick up the cushions and find it. Once, I found nearly two dollars in quarters and dimes."

I laughed. "Your secret's safe with me," I told him. I leaned over and kissed him on the forehead. For a moment, he looked so shocked I thought he might cry or scream. When I turned around, I saw the cause of his alarm. Uncle Reuben was standing in the doorway.

"What the hell are you two doing in here?" Uncle Reuben's face was bright red with fury. "Raven, get away from my son. I knew you were a no-good troublemaker like your mother. And here you are flaunting yourself around and tempting my son just the way she tempted me. Well, I won't have none of it! Get out of this room right now before I drag you out!" For a second, I was too terrified to move. Then Uncle Reuben started pulling William toward him, and I knew I had to get away.

I saw William's horrified face as I ran past him and knew that I had to speak up.

"We didn't do anything, Uncle Reuben. Honest, William was just showing me his birdhouses." I was probably just making him more furious, but I had no idea why he had gotten so angry, and I was ashamed that I was leaving William to face his father's fury all alone.

Not stopping to look back, I ran downstairs and straight into my room, shutting the door tightly behind me. I knew that Uncle Reuben would break down the door if he wanted to, but the house was quiet suddenly, and I prayed that maybe I was safe. For now.

I tried to start on my math homework, but there was no way I could concentrate with my heart still racing and my pulse pounding. What if Uncle Reuben was upstairs hurting William? What did he think we were doing, anyway?

William already lived in constant fear of being ridiculed and belittled by his father, and now it seemed that Uncle Reuben had one more thing to add to his ammunition — against both of us.

It was obvious even to me that the reason William was so withdrawn was that he was afraid. Afraid that he would get yelled at, made fun of, or maybe even worse. I knew Aunt Clara was concerned about William; she even talked about taking him to a doctor. Why couldn't she see that the reason William was so quiet and timid was that he was afraid?

What would happen if I stayed in this house where I was belittled and ridiculed as well — for my birth, for my mother, for things I hadn't even done? Would I become like William? Would I just one day disappear inside myself?

Just as I was opening my math book, Aunt Clara poked her head in the door. "Raven, are you all right?" Her eyes were all red and puffy, and I could see that she'd been crying.

"Yes, Aunt Clara, I'm fine. How is William? Uncle Reuben didn't hurt him, did he? We weren't doing anything bad, Aunt Clara! I was just thanking William for showing me his birdhouses. We . . . we . . ." Talking about it made me upset all over again, and I began sobbing so hard I couldn't even speak.

Aunt Clara came to sit beside me on the bed. "Shh . . . I know, dear, I know. Everything will be fine."

"But, but William . . . what did Uncle Reuben do to him?" Why wasn't she answering my questions?

"He's fine, dear, but please, promise me not to speak of this again. Reuben will just get upset all over again. Promise me you won't speak of it!"

"I promise, Aunt Clara."

She stood there for a few moments, then told me not to stay up too late studying, and left. I sat with my math book on my lap and stared up at the dark ceiling. I could hear Uncle Reuben's heavy footsteps, a door close, water running, and a phone ringing. Poor William, I thought. I had seen it in his face. He was terrified. What about Aunt Clara? Had she built a wall of self-denial around herself, shutting up the dark secrets? Like a coiled fuse attached to a time bomb, sooner or later all the horror in this house was sure to explode.

I didn't want to be here before. I surely didn't want to be here now, but what choice did I have? I had no father. I had no other relatives. I felt trapped, caged in by events far beyond my control. It heightened the panic that throbbed so loudly in my heart, I thought for sure it sounded like a jungle drum beating out the rhythms of alarm.

What should I pray for? My mother's miraculous appearance? My mystery father's sudden interest in a daughter he had never known? Who was more lost than me, someone without even a real name, forced to live with people who really didn't want me?

A real rumble of thunder pounded at the windowpane and was soon followed by a downpour. Thick raindrops tapped at the window as the wind grew stronger, slapping torrents against the walls. I heard Aunt Clara rushing around downstairs shutting windows. Then I heard Uncle Reuben curse from the top of the stairs. Moments later, it was silent except for the monotonous sound of drizzle. I could feel the darkness deepening around me, wrapping itself around this house.

My cheeks felt cold. All my tears had turned to ice behind my eyes. I turned over and buried my face in the pillow as I tightened myself into the fetal position and swallowed back my fear and loneliness.

Sunlight fell on my face and woke me up just as Uncle Reuben was coming down the stairs. I flew off the bed and hurried to the bathroom. Even before I could wash my face, he was bellowing about my not being in the kitchen helping Aunt Clara prepare breakfast for everyone. It looked as if things were back to normal.

"Why weren't you up and helping?" Uncle Reuben demanded.

William entered and took his seat at the table. His eyes met mine for a moment before he looked down at his cereal and juice.

Uncle Reuben looked from William to me and slammed his fist down on the table. "I don't ever want to catch you in William's room again, understand?"

"Yes," I said, hoping that that would be the last said about last night.

"And today, again, I got to take time out of my busy schedule to look into your problems. I bet your mother never spent a minute on you. Did she ever go to the school to see how you were doing?"

I sat and began to sip my orange juice.

"When I speak to you, I want you to look at me and respond," he ordered.

"No, she never did," I said.

"I didn't think so," he said, pleased with my answer. He looked at Aunt Clara, who kept busy at the sink.

"Jennifer should come down, Reuben. She'll be late for the bus."

"She's never late," he said.

"You know she has been a few times, and you had to drive her to school," Aunt Clara said softly.

"The bus came too early those days," he insisted.

By the time Jennifer appeared, William and I had finished eating. I began to clear the table.

"Leave that," Jennifer ordered when I reached for the sugar bowl. "I haven't had my cereal yet."

"You should get up earlier, Jennifer," Aunt Clara said. "You don't have much time."

"I would if I could find the clothes I

want," Jennifer whined. "Someone put my blouses in the wrong place, and my favorite skirt was shoved so far in the back of the closet I nearly didn't find it." She glared at me.

"You could put your clothes away yourself, and that way you'd know where everything is," I said.

"You're just jealous because I have more clothes than you. If you had as many as I did, you'd have trouble remembering where you put them," she said angrily. "Besides, you probably were hiding this skirt so you could wear it."

"I don't want to wear your things. I have my own clothes and . . ."

"Stop this bickering at the table!" Uncle Reuben shouted. He rose out of his seat like a gusher, his face crimson and steaming. Jennifer sat, and Aunt Clara quickly poured some coffee in a cup for her. "We never had bickering at the table before," he added, glaring at me, "but I bet that was something that happened in your house often."

"It wasn't," I said.

Aunt Clara glanced at me fearfully and shook her head gently. She wanted me to be like her, bury my head in the sand, absorb Uncle Reuben's hateful remarks, and pray that it would all end quickly.

"If I do anything of any value for you, it will be to teach you how to behave properly," he continued. "I know there are years of degenerate living to overcome, but by God, if you're going to live with us, you'll overcome them," he said, wagging his monstrous fist at me. "Why don't you watch Jennifer? Learn from her," he suggested.

I raised my eyebrows and nearly laughed. Jennifer sat there smugly, chomping down on a few flakes of cereal, sipping some coffee before jumping up.

"We've got to go, Daddy," she declared. "You can teach her how to behave later."

He grunted. William looked at me sympathetically but said nothing. I went to get my books and left the house a few seconds after Jennifer. She was already down the sidewalk, meeting her friends at the bus stop. The big topic of conversation was the upcoming school dance. The girls were all talking about which boys they hoped would ask them. Jennifer's wish list was the longest.

"She hasn't been here long, but do you think anyone will ask her?" I heard Paula Gordon whisper as she nodded in my direction.

"Who would ask her?" Jennifer said, loud enough for me to hear, and she laughed.

"Oh, no, wait a minute. Maybe Clarence Dunsen will ask her."

"Yeah," Paula said. "He'll go, 'Raven, would . . . would . . . wouldwouldwould . . . would . . . you . . . you . . . like to . . . to . . . gogogo . . . ' "

They laughed loudly and then moved away. Their voices grew softer, more secretive. I was relieved to see the bus pull up. I hurried on. They all laughed again when they filed past and looked at me sitting with Clarence.

Funny, I thought, how girls like Jennifer attract other girls just like her. They stick together as comfortably as a pig in its own mess, I thought. It made me laugh. Clarence looked at me with curiosity. For a moment, I wished he would ask me to the dance and we would show them all up. But that was a fantasy, and in my life, fantasies were written on clouds that floated by, impossible to grasp, caught in the wind, gone as fast as they appeared.

6

He Likes Me!

I had a crush on a boy when I was in the sixth
grade. His name was Ronnie Clark, and he
had blue eyes that brightened with so much
warmth when he smiled that he made you
feel good when you were upset, and yet his
eyes could darken with mystery and intensity
when he looked at someone intensely or was
in deep thought. I caught him gazing at me
that way a few times, and it made my heart
flutter and sent tiny warm jolts of electricity
up and down my spine. Suddenly, I thought
about my hair, my clothes, a budding pimple
on my chin.

The world around you changes when you
realize someone as handsome as Ronnie
Clark is gazing at you with interest. Every
time I moved or turned, when I rose to walk
out of the classroom, even when I picked up

my pen to write in my notebook, I was very conscious of how I looked. I couldn't wait to get to a mirror to check my face and my hair. I hated my clothes and regretted not watching my mother do her makeup when she did it well.

I tried not to be obvious when I looked at Ronnie, and if he caught me looking, I always shifted my eyes quickly and pretended I didn't have the slightest interest in him. Sometimes he smiled, and sometimes he looked disappointed. He was as shy as I was, and I thought it would take a bulldozer to push us dramatically into each other's path. He didn't seem to have the nerve to sit next to me in the cafeteria or come up to me in the hallway, and after a while, I was afraid that I might be making more of his gazes than there was. Nothing could be more embarrassing than thinking a boy liked you when he didn't.

One afternoon, when I was in gym class, I looked at the doorway to the gymnasium and saw him standing there looking my way. We were playing volleyball, and we were all in our gym outfits. The ball bounced close to the doorway, and I chased it and seized it, looking up at him at the same time.

"Nice," he said.

Butterflies panicked in my chest, but I

gave him the best smile I could muster. Mrs. Wilson blew her whistle and shouted for me to get back into the game. Ronnie walked away quickly before she chastised him for being there, but at lunch, he came up to me in the line and told me I was pretty good at volleyball.

"You could probably be on the girls' team now instead of waiting another year," he said.

"Tell me what it's like to be on a school team," I asked him, and he followed me to the table.

We started dating soon after that, but never did much more than hold hands and kiss a few times after school. I met him at the movies one night, but he had to go home right afterward. And then, just as suddenly as it had all started, it ended. He turned away from me as if I had been just another interesting picture in a museum. Soon he was off looking at other girls the way he'd once looked at me. I felt stupid chasing after him, so I stopped looking for him, and that was about when my school attendance began to drop off anyway.

There were many fewer students at the school I now attended and only about a dozen or so boys I would consider as good-looking as Ronnie Clark. I agreed with Jennifer that I could never expect any of them to take any interest in me, but to my surprise that very afternoon after Jennifer and her friends had teased me about Clarence Dunsen, a chubby boy named Gary Carson bumped into me deliberately between classes, and when I turned to complain, he smiled and said, "Jimmy Freer likes you."

He hurried on, leaving me confused. I knew who Jimmy Freer was. He was captain of the junior varsity basketball team, tall for his age, and very, very good-looking. He was right at the top of Jennifer's wish list, and I never even dreamed he would be looking at me, but at lunch he was suddenly right behind me when I went to buy some milk.

"That's the healthy choice," he quipped. I turned and, for a moment, was too surprised to speak. "Most everyone else is buying soda."

"I don't drink much soda," I told him. "Milk's okay." I paid for my milk and headed for the table where Terri and some of the other girls I liked were sitting, but he caught up with me.

"How about sitting with me?" he asked, and nodded toward an empty table on our right.

I gazed at the girls, who were all looking my way with interest, and then I turned and saw Jennifer and her friends staring at me, too. It warmed my heart to see the jealousy in their faces and made me smile.

"Okay," I said. He led the way and set his tray down across from me.

"How do you like the school here?" he asked, dipping his spoon into his bowl of chicken rice soup.

"It's okay."

"Is that your favorite word?" he joked.

"No. Sometimes I say it's not okay."

He laughed, and I noticed what a nice smile he had and what a perfectly straight nose. I liked the way a small dimple in his right cheek appeared when he talked. His dark brown hair was cut closely on the sides, but he let a wave sweep back from the front. He had beautiful hazel eyes, bejeweled with flecks of blue, green, and gold on soft brown. No wonder he was everyone's heart-throb, I thought, and tried to look cool and sophisticated under his gaze. I could feel the way everyone was looking at us in the cafeteria. It made me think I was on a big television screen and every little move I made was magnified. I brushed my lips quickly with my napkin, afraid a crumb might be on my mouth or chin.

"So you're living with Jennifer, huh?" he asked.

"Sort of," I said.

"Sort of?"

"I don't call it living," I told him, and he laughed again. Then he smiled, his eyes drinking me in so intently I felt as if I were sitting there naked.

"I had a feeling you were smarter than most of the girls in junior high school here."

"I'm hardly smarter."

"You know what I mean," he said with that impish gleam in his eyes.

"No, I don't."

He laughed and grew serious. "Have you been to any school basketball games yet?"

"No."

"There's a big one coming up tomorrow night with Roscoe. We beat them once, and they beat us once this year. Why don't you come?" he asked.

"I don't know if I can."

"Why can't you? Don't you believe in having school spirit?" he asked with that teasing smile returning.

"It's not that. I don't know if my uncle will let me out," I said.

He grew serious-looking and ate as he thought.

"Why?" He leaned toward me to whisper.

"Did you have a bad record at the last school you attended or something?"

"Sure. I'm on the post office walls everywhere," I said. He stared a moment and then roared so hard that kids who were sitting nearby stopped talking to look at us.

"You really are something. Come on, come to the game. Afterward, Missy Taylor is having a small house party. We'll have a good time, especially if we beat Roscoe. Can I hear you say okay again?"

"I can't make any promises," I said, but I really wanted to go.

"You're old enough to go out if you want. They shouldn't keep you locked up. Jennifer's certainly not kept locked up," he added. "She'll be at the game, I bet. You can come with her, can't you?"

"I'll try," I said. "She's not happy about taking me along anywhere."

"I'll make sure she does," he said with a wink.

We talked some more. He asked questions about my life before I began living with Uncle Reuben. I didn't want to tell him too much. Jennifer had successfully spread the word that my mother had died, and for the moment, I was afraid to contradict her and create too much of a scandal. It might scare Jimmy away, I thought, and anyway, what difference did it make what the kids at this school knew or didn't know about me?

Jennifer approached me in the hallway the first opportunity she had after lunch. Normally, she wouldn't so much as glance in my direction, but her girlfriends were buzzing around her like bees full of curiosity instead of honey.

"What's going on between you and Jimmy?" she demanded as if she were a police interrogator. She stood in front of me with her hands on her hips.

"Excuse me," I said. "I don't want to be late for class."

"Don't you walk away from me, Raven," she cried, her nostrils flaring. She looked exactly like Uncle Reuben.

"I'm not walking away. Do you want me to be late and get into trouble? Uncle Reuben won't like that, will he?"

"You've got time. Answer me," she demanded.

"Jimmy who?" I said, looking perplexed.

"Jimmy who? Jimmy Freer. You were talking to him in the cafeteria," she said, amazed at my questions. She looked at the other girls, who were just as surprised.

"Oh," I said, "was that his name? He never told me. Um . . . nothing's going on, but when something is, you'll be the first to know," I added, and kept walking. I could almost hear the explosion of anger in her head.

I didn't realize that because I had been seen with Jimmy Freer, Jennifer was going to pay more attention to me. She was even waiting for me at the bus at the end of the day.

"Do you want to go to the basketball game tomorrow night?" she asked in as close to a pleasant voice as she could speak.

"What?"

"Are you deaf? I asked you if you wanted to go to the game with me, that's all."

"Sure," I said. Now I was the one who was really surprised.

"Just don't get my father angry about anything and spoil it," she warned, and marched onto the bus before I could ask her why she suddenly didn't mind being seen with me. I found out later. One of Jimmy's friends, Brad Dillon, had asked Jennifer to the game and party. The plan was to double-date with me and Jimmy, and since Brad was on Jennifer's wish list, she was eager to get me to go and make it happen for herself. I was more surprised that Brad wanted to be with her. He was even better-looking than Jimmy, in my opinion, but as we would soon discover, the boys had their own special plans.

Jennifer really wanted this date. All that evening and the next day, she did everything she could to ensure that Uncle Reuben wouldn't stop us from attending the game. I was suddenly very important to her. She even offered to help with some of the chores and put on a big act of reconciliation, pretending to help me make friends.

Uncle Reuben had made an appointment at the social service agency and announced at dinner that he was undertaking the necessary steps to make himself my formal legal guardian. In the meantime, social services was promising to cover my health and basic needs.

"It still irks me that society has to pay for my sister's mistakes," he declared as he chomped down on a lamb chop. I thought he would consume it, bone and all, like some bulldog.

I looked up sharply. It was as if he had reached across the table and poked me with his fork.

"I'm not a mistake," I said as proudly as I could. I was a tight wire inside, stretched so tautly I thought I might break and cry, but I held my breath and kept a firm lid on my well of tears.

Uncle Reuben paused and glared at me, the meat caught between his thick lips and the grease gleaming on his chin. Jennifer looked up nervously. Aunt Clara held her breath, and William gazed down at his food. I could almost feel the trembling in his little body.

"It's a mistake not to be prepared properly for children," he said firmly.

"My mother made mistakes, but I'm not a mistake. I'm a human being with feelings, too." I tossed my hair back. "Nobody's perfect, anyway."

"You hear that? You hear the way she talks and thinks? You'd think she would be more respectful and grateful. Here I am trying to make a new home for her, and she talks like that, insolent."

"I'm not being insolent, Uncle Reuben."

"She didn't mean it," Jennifer piped up.

Uncle Reuben raised his eyebrows and gazed at her. Even I had to pause and look at her. She flashed me a quick look of warning.

"It's hard to start in a new school with new people. I'm going to help her make new friends," Jennifer offered.

Aunt Clara beamed. "That's wonderful, dear. You see, Reuben, the girls will get along just fine."

He still had a glint of suspicion in his eyes,

but he grunted and continued to eat. Jennifer began talking about the basketball game as if it was the event of the century.

"Even our teachers are going to attend. It's important to show school spirit."

"That's very nice," Aunt Clara said.

Uncle Reuben started to talk about his own school days, and for a moment, I felt as if I was really sitting at a family dinner. Aunt Clara even laughed, recalling some stories he described, but then he suddenly stopped and looked at William.

"You hear how important it is to participate in sports, William. You shouldn't spend so much time in your room. You should stay after school sometimes and join a team," he told him.

William gazed at me with desperately sad eyes.

"He's too young. They don't have teams yet," I said.

"Sure they do," Uncle Reuben snapped. "He wouldn't even go out for the Little League when he had the chance. I was going to drag him over to the field, but his mother was too upset."

"Not everyone has to be an athlete. Some people have other talents. William is fantastic at building things," I said.

"What is this? You're not here a month,

and you're telling me what my son is capable of doing and not capable of doing?" Uncle Reuben cried. "She's just like my sister, with a mouth bigger than her brain. When I say something to William, I don't want to hear you contradict it, understand?" he said, slamming his fork down on the table.

"She didn't mean anything," Jennifer said quickly. "Raven, if you want, I'll help you with the dishes, and then we'll work on your math. I told you I would help you," she said, turning her back on Uncle Reuben and winking at me.

I shook my head and went back to eating. After dinner, when Uncle Reuben retired to the living room to watch television, Jennifer did help with the dishes. She stood beside me at the sink and whispered.

"Can't you keep your big mouth shut at dinner? Just let Daddy make his speeches like I do, and don't say anything," she advised.

"He bullies this family," I remarked.

"Who cares? You want him to get angry and forbid us to go to the game and the party? Just shut up." She wiped another dish and then turned and left the kitchen.

Where was the love in this house? I wondered. What makes this more of a family than what I had with my mother? Was it just the roof over their heads and the food in the refrigerator? I was beginning to think I would rather settle for the occasional good days with Mama than the constant life of tension and fear that existed in this home, but I didn't even have the choice anymore. Maybe I truly was a mistake. I was someone who could be moved and ordered about like a piece of furniture.

The next day at school, Jimmy paid even more attention to me. He walked with me in the halls between classes and sat with me at lunch. When I asked him if Brad Dillon really wanted to go out with my cousin, he just smiled and said, "I told you I would make sure you got to the game, didn't I? Let's just have a good time. I'll be looking in the bleachers for you," he promised.

Jennifer talked Uncle Reuben into driving us to the school gymnasium. It wasn't until we were almost there that she revealed we were invited to a party after the game. He almost stopped and turned around to take us home.

"What do you mean? What party?" He bellowed so loudly I thought the windows would shatter.

I sat quietly in the backseat and listened to Jennifer rattle off her lies.

"Everyone's going. It's a chaperoned party at Missy Taylor's house. We won't be late. It's a celebration," she explained.

"How come you didn't say anything about it before?" he demanded.

"We just got invited, right, Raven? Missy called us."

I didn't say anything. He wasn't going to blame me later. I was determined about that. I saw his eyes go to the rearview mirror.

"Who's this Missy Taylor?"

"Melissa Taylor. You know her father. He owns Taylor's Steak House."

"That's no more than a bar," Uncle Reuben said.

"They have a nice house," Jennifer continued.

He grunted. "I don't want you home late. Be home before twelve. How are you getting home, anyway?" he asked.

"Oh, we have a ride. Don't worry, Daddy."

He looked at her again and then at me through the mirror. "I'm not happy about this. Who's the chaperone?"

"Her mother's there. Stop worrying so much, Daddy. You went to parties when you were our age."

"No, I didn't. I didn't even go out on a

real date until I was a senior."

This time, I grunted, unable to imagine anyone going out on a date with him. He looked at me through the mirror again and drove on.

It was a very exciting game. Jimmy was spectacular, stealing the ball, making long shots, holding the team together, and keeping them within four points the whole time. He did what he promised, too: he looked into the bleachers and found me. When he smiled, Jennifer glanced at me with eyes so green with hot envy I thought she would burst into flames.

In the last minute of the game, Jimmy intercepted a pass and scored. Then one of their players was fouled but missed his shot. The ball was tossed to Jimmy, who made a long jump shot from the corner. It put the game into two-minute overtime. The crowd was excited, and the roar was deafening. When they stomped their feet, I thought the bleachers would come tumbling down and crush us all.

The overtime was just as exciting as the game, each team scoring until the last thirty seconds, when Jimmy had an opportunity to score and delayed it as long as possible. The crowd held its collective breath as the ball sailed through the air and threaded through the basket to give our school the victory. The team carried Jimmy off the court, the school's hero.

"And you're going to be with him at the party!" Paula Gordon moaned.

"I have no idea why," I said.

She exchanged a funny look with Jennifer, both covering their smiles with their hands.

Afterward, the boys joined us to watch the varsity game, but it wasn't as exciting, and during the halftime, Jimmy suggested we just leave and go to the party.

"We'll get a head start," he said.

We piled into two cars and headed for Missy Taylor's house. The weather had turned bad, and there was a constant drizzle, but rather than put a damper on our excitement, it made everyone squeal and scream as we rushed to get into the automobiles. When we arrived at the house, I discovered both her parents were at their bar and restaurant, so Jennifer's first lie was immediately evident. It was a nice house, bigger than Uncle Reuben and Aunt Clara's. Missy was an only child, and there were four bedrooms as well as a basement party room with a bar and a jukebox.

The music started immediately, and Brad got behind the bar and began to pour beer and vodka. I didn't want to drink anything, but everyone was drinking, even Jennifer, who claimed she was used to drinking vodka.

"I drink it at home and then put water in the bottle so my father won't know," she said. I actually believed her, but it wasn't long before she began to feel sick and had to go to the bathroom to throw up.

"She drank it too fast," Jimmy said. "That's the trick, drinking slowly. You're doing all right. You know how to handle yourself, I see."

I had only sipped half a glass of beer. My mother would roar with laughter, I thought.

"Come on," Jimmy said, taking my hand. "Let's leave these losers behind."

"Where are we going?"

"You'll see," he said. He led me up the stairway to the bedroom.

"We can't just walk through her house like this, can we?" I asked.

"Sure, Missy knows. It's all right," he said. "We've had parties here before. It's a great party house, because her parents don't keep track of what we drink, and they're always out."

Missy Taylor can't have much of a family, either, I thought. I was beginning to wonder if any of the kids at school were really better off than me.

Jimmy did seem to know exactly where to go. He led me to one of the guest bedrooms. As soon as we passed through the door, he kicked it closed and embraced me. It was the most wonderful kiss I had ever experienced, long, wet, and so hard it made the back of my neck ache. As he kissed me, he brought his hands up the sides of my body to my shoulders and then kissed my neck.

"You're delicious," he said. "Just as I imagined you would be."

"I'm not something to eat," I said, trying to laugh. I was getting very nervous. I liked him, wanted him to kiss me, but he was moving so fast he made my heart pound. His hands were on my breasts, and his fingers were manipulating the buttons of my blouse. As he did that, he walked us toward the bed, and before I knew it, we were sitting on it. He brought his lips to my chest and began to work on my bra.

"Wait," I said.

"For what?"

"I don't want to do this so fast. We can get in trouble," I told him.

He looked at me with a frozen smile on his lips. "Don't worry. We won't. I have what we need. You expected I would, didn't you?"

"What? No," I said.

"What do you mean, no? You agreed to

come here with me. What did you think we'd be doing, having popcorn and watching television? You know what's happening, and I know about you. Jennifer's told everyone."

"What?" I pushed him back. "What did she tell everyone?"

"Hey, what's going on? This isn't brain surgery. We're just having a good time. You've had them before."

"Not like this," I said, standing. "I don't know what Jennifer has told everyone, but I'm not what you think."

"Come on," he said. "I don't kiss and tell." He reached for my hand, and I stepped back.

"Neither do I," I said. "I'm nobody's one-night stand," I added, repeating something Mama had once told one of her lovers. As it turned out, she was often a one-night stand.

"I thought you were cooler than the girls here," he said. "Why do you think I asked you out on the night of the biggest game? Come on," he said, reaching for me again. "Don't I deserve some reward?"

"No," I said. "You deserve a kick between the legs, and that's what you're going to get if you try to pull me onto that bed," I threatened. My eyes were full of fire.

He cowered. "Fine. Get the hell out, then."

I headed for the door.

"You and your cousin are full of it," he yelled after me.

"Don't put me in the same category as Jennifer," I spit back, disgusted.

Out in the hallway, I saw Brad leaving one of the bedrooms, a smile on his face as he hurried to straighten his clothes.

"Brad, where's Jennifer? We're going home!"

"Fine, chill, I'm done with her. She's all yours." He laughed as he made his way downstairs to the party.

I pushed open the bedroom door and saw Jennifer lying on the bed, her skirt bunched up and her shirt halfway unbuttoned. She looked as if she was sleeping, but I had enough experience with my mother to know that she was passed out.

"Jennifer, wake up!" I shouted, shaking her by the shoulder. "C'mon, we've got to get out of here!"

"What? Who? Raven . . . what are you doing here? What happened?" She looked groggily around the room. "Where's Brad? We were having fun, and then the room started to spin, and I . . ."

"Come *on*, Jennifer, you have to get up!" I

pulled her into a sitting position, and she swung her legs over the side of the bed.

"Ohhh, my head! I want to go home," she moaned, clutching the side of the bed.

"We will. That's why I came looking for you. But first you better tell me what kind of stories you've been telling everyone about me," I demanded.

"Please, Raven, I just want to go home."

I could tell there was no use talking to her in this condition, so I put my arm around her and helped her to the stairs. Brad was standing at the foot of the stairs with a group of boys, and they were all laughing hysterically.

"Somebody better take us home," I said. "Jennifer's sick. We need to go now."

"Why don't you just hitchhike?" Brad suggested. Everyone laughed.

Jennifer and I made our way downstairs, and I turned to Missy Taylor who had come up from the basement to see what all the laughing was about.

"If someone doesn't take us home, my uncle will make a lot of trouble for you, especially with all this drinking going on."

She smirked. "Take them home, Brad. I don't want to get into trouble. They're too young to be here, anyway. It was a stupid idea."

"I'll say it was," Jimmy piped up from behind us.

"Come on," I urged Jennifer, and we walked to the front door.

"Let's get moving," Brad said angrily. "I don't want to miss the fun."

"Yes, we'd hate to have you miss any of the fun. Some fun," I muttered, and led Jennifer to his car. She sprawled out in the backseat.

"She better not throw up in my car," Brad said.

"You really didn't want to bring her here. Why did you?"

"I did it as a favor for Jimmy so you would come. I guess you didn't hit it off, huh?" he said, smiling. "That's okay, though, Jennifer and I had fun." Jennifer giggled from the backseat.

"No," I said, "we didn't hit it off."

"A lot of girls want to go out with Jimmy," he said as if I had lost a golden opportunity.

"Here's one who doesn't," I said.

He shook his head. "Man, where are you from?" he asked.

Yes, where am I from? I wondered, and then I thought, it doesn't matter where I'm from. It's where I'm going that matters.

7

The Party's Over

It was raining harder when we arrived home. Brad wouldn't help me with Jennifer. He just sat there waiting impatiently while I struggled to get her out of the car. She didn't even seem to realize we were getting soaked, because she wouldn't or couldn't move quickly. I practically carried her from Brad's car to the house. He shot off as soon as we were out of the automobile. By the time we reached the door, both of us were soaked. I had hoped to sneak Jennifer in and up to her room, but the moment I opened the front door, Uncle Reuben sprang from his recliner in the living room and appeared in the hallway. His eyes bulged when he saw Jennifer. She was pale, her clothes wet and disheveled, her hair messed with strands sticking to her forehead, and her eyes half closed. She leaned on me for support, and I guided her into the house.

"What the hell happened to her? What's wrong?" he demanded. "Is she sick?"

She lifted her eyes and looked at him pathetically for a moment and then suddenly burst out laughing and crying at the same time.

He turned to me. "What's going on here?"

"She drank some vodka at the party," I said. I had made up my mind I wouldn't lie to protect her.

"What? Drank some . . . Clara!" he screamed.

Aunt Clara came rushing out of the bedroom and appeared at the top of the stairway. She wore only her nightgown. "What is it, Reuben?"

"Look at your daughter," he declared, extending his arms toward Jennifer.

She looked even more ridiculous wearing an idiotic smile and clinging to my arm. Her eyes rolled, and she pressed her hands to her stomach. "Uh-oh. I don't feel so good," she moaned.

Uncle Reuben turned to me again. "I thought you said the party was chaperoned."

"I didn't say anything. That was Jennifer," I said.

He curled his thick, dark eyebrows toward each other and narrowed his eyes into slits of suspicion. "Who gave her the vodka?"

"I'm sick, Daddy. Let me go upstairs," she pleaded.

"Oh, dear, dear," Aunt Clara cried, coming down the stairs quickly. She took Jennifer's other arm. We started toward the stairway, but Uncle Reuben reached out with his large hands and grasped my shoulders, pulling me away and toward him. He nearly lifted me off the floor as he brought his nose closer to my face and sniffed.

"You drank something, too," he accused.

"Just half a glass of beer," I said.

"I knew it. I just knew this sort of thing would happen when you came into my home."

"It wasn't my fault," I cried, and pushed his hand away from my shoulder. "Jennifer wanted to go to this party more than I did. And she knew exactly what was going to be happening there," I told him. If he only knew what else had happened — even his precious princess wouldn't be safe from his wrath.

He didn't hear a word. Jennifer stumbled on a step, and Aunt Clara struggled to keep her from falling. Uncle Reuben shot forward, scooped Jennifer up in his arms, and charged up the stairway with her as if she were nothing more than a toddler.

"Don't shake her so much, Reuben," Aunt Clara warned, climbing after them. It was too late. Jennifer started heaving again just as he reached the upstairs landing. He hurried toward the bathroom.

"Oh, dear, dear," Aunt Clara said, pressing her hands together and then to her face. She paused to look at me and shook her head. "How could this happen, Raven?"

"I think it's happened before, Aunt Clara, only you never knew," I said. I wasn't sure exactly what had happened with Jennifer and Brad, or if it had happened before with other boys, but I was pretty sure Jennifer wouldn't want her parents to know about that, either.

She bit down on her lip and started upstairs. Uncle Reuben stepped out of the bathroom.

"See to her," he ordered. "Give her a cold shower."

William had come to the doorway of his bedroom dressed in his pajamas. He wiped his eyes and looked out at the bedlam, confused. "What's going on?" he asked.

"Go back to sleep," Uncle Reuben ordered. Then he turned to glare down at me.

"I want to talk to you," he charged.

"I didn't do anything," I protested, and went to my little room, closing the door behind me.

He nearly ripped it off the hinges opening it again. "Don't you dare walk away from me!" he screamed.

"It wasn't my fault, Uncle Reuben. She wanted to go to the game and the party. She talked the boys into asking us. She went right to the bar and poured herself a glass of vodka, claiming she knew how to drink, but she got sick right away. I guess she drank too much too fast trying to show off. I brought her home as soon as I could. That's the truth."

"Jennifer never went to a party like that before," he insisted. "She's never come home like this. Somehow, I'm sure this was all your doing."

"Believe what you want," I said. "You will anyway."

I turned my back on him. It was a big mistake. Seconds later, his big left hand was at my neck, and his right hand scooped up the hem of my dress. He lifted me off the floor and tossed me to the pullout, nearly knocking it over with me on it. Before I could scream, he had unbuckled his belt and pulled it off his pants. The next thing I knew, he was pulling down my panties. Then I screamed as loud and as hard as I could.

"Bitch!" he said. "Bad seed! You're not coming here and ruining my Jennifer. I'll put an end to this bad behavior right now."

The first whack of the belt shocked me more than it hurt me. I couldn't believe this was happening. With his large palm on my back, he held me down as he swung his belt again. This time, the pain shot up my spine.

"Wagging your rear at boys, going to parties, drinking and who knows what else. You are just like your mother," he said. "You should have been whipped before this, but it's not too late. No, sir." He hit me again and then again. Between my screams and my tears, I started to choke. It was useless to try to get away. He as much as nailed me to the bed with his heavy palm. He finally stopped beating me, but for a long moment he just held me down. My rear end was stinging in pain. It was as if I had been stung by dozens of wasps. I felt him move his right hand over it, but this time surprisingly softly. I wondered if he was checking to be sure he had done enough damage. Then he pulled his left hand from my back. I was afraid to turn, afraid to move. I sensed him standing there, gazing down at me, breathing hard.

"Maybe now you'll behave," he said.

I shuddered with sobs and heard him leave, closing the door behind him. For a long time, I didn't move. I remained there, with my face down, waiting for the pain to subside. Finally, it did so enough for me to turn over. It hurt to move my legs and even more to put pressure on my rear. I sprawled on my back and tried to catch my breath, wiping my face. I think I was bothered more by my outrage and loss of dignity than the stinging and aching, however. Slowly, I leaned over and pulled my panties back on. When I stood up, it was like rising from a beach or poolside and realizing you had been sunburned. My skin was throbbing, and there was a deep, sick feeling in the center of my stomach.

I wanted to open the door and scream, "How dare you do this to me?"

I actually did open it, but when I looked out at the quiet house, I suddenly became even more terrified. If he would do this, who knew what else he would do? Instead, I made my way to the bathroom and tried putting a warm, damp towel on my battered thighs and rear.

It didn't help much. I returned to my

room, moving cautiously and slowly through the house. I could hear Uncle Reuben yelling upstairs and Aunt Clara's muffled sobs. I barely had enough strength to undress, and when I finally did lie down, the throbbing grew worse. It kept me awake most of the night. I think I passed out rather than fell asleep sometime just before morning.

A cold shock woke me, and I realized I was drenched in ice water. I cried out and sat up to face Uncle Reuben, who stood there with the emptied pail in his hands. The water quickly soaked right through the blanket, but I kept it close to my half-naked body.

"You get yourself up and get out there to help Clara do the weekly cleaning," he demanded. "You won't sleep late here because you carried on like a tramp, hear? I'll teach you what it means to misbehave while living with me," he threatened, speaking through clenched teeth. "I'm not your mother. None of this goes here. Now, get up!"

"I will. Leave me alone," I moaned.

He started to throw more water on me.

"Reuben, stop!" Aunt Clara cried from the hallway.

He glared at me and then nodded and left

the room, pausing at the doorway to speak to Aunt Clara.

"Don't baby her, Clara. She needs strict discipline. She's no more than a wild animal."

He walked off.

When I began to move, the pain from my beaten body shot up my spine and made me cry out.

"What is it?" Aunt Clara said, coming in. "What's wrong, Raven?"

"He beat me, Aunt Clara. He beat me with a belt last night."

She shook her head in denial, but I turned on my side and lifted the blanket from my legs and rear. Then she gasped and stepped back. "Oh, dear, dear."

"Is it bad?"

"It's inflamed, welts," she cried. "Reuben, how could you do such a thing?" she asked, but far from loudly enough for him to hear. It was more as if she was asking herself how her husband could have turned into such a monster. There were other questions to ask, but this was hardly the time to suggest them, I thought.

"I'll get some balm," she said. "Just stay there, Raven. Oh, dear, dear," she muttered, and hurried out.

I collapsed back onto the pillow, my head

pounding. What tortured me was not the beating I had been unfairly given as much as the realization that there was no one I could depend on now that Mama had gotten herself into even deeper trouble. Aunt Clara was too weak. I had no other relatives to run to for help. I was in a strange town in a school where I was still so new that I hadn't had time to make close friends. I was truly trapped.

"Here, dear. Let me see what I can do," Aunt Clara said, hurrying back.

I turned over to let her apply the medicine. It did bring some cool relief.

"I can't believe he did this," she muttered. "But he was so upset. He has such a temper."

"I didn't make Jennifer drink the vodka, Aunt Clara. Those kids are all her friends, not mine."

"I know, dear. I know."

"He won't believe anything bad about her," I said, turning when she was finished. She stared at me. "It's not fair, and it's not right," I continued.

"I'll speak to him," she promised, nodding.

"It won't matter, Aunt Clara. He has a bad opinion of me and my mother, and he hates me for being alive and a problem for you. I should just leave."

"Of course not. Where would you go? Don't even think of such a thing, Raven. He'll calm down. Everything will be all right," she insisted, just as someone living in Never-Never Land would.

"It won't be all right. He'll never calm down," I said. "He's an ogre. He's more than that. I know why he favors Jennifer so much, too," I added, more under my breath. Aunt Clara either didn't hear me or pretended not to. She quickly turned away.

"I'll make us some hot breakfast, and we'll all feel better. You take your time, dear. Take your time," she said, and left before I could add a word.

I sat there fuming. All I wanted to do was get my hands on Jennifer and wring her neck until she confessed the truth. I wasn't going to let her get away with this, I thought. I took the beating that should have been meant for her.

I stepped out cautiously, hating even the thought of facing Uncle Reuben now. I heard no voices, just the clanking of dishes and the sounds of Aunt Clara moving about the kitchen. When I peered in, I saw William alone at the table. Jennifer was permitted to sleep off the effects of last night, but not me.

Anger raged up in me like milk simmering too long in a pot. I felt the heat rise into my face. Without hesitation, I turned and started up the stairs. If I had to drag her down these steps and throw her at her father's feet, babbling the truth, I would do it, I thought.

As I turned at the landing, I saw that her bedroom door was slightly ajar. I started for it and stopped when I heard the distinct sound of whimpering. Then I heard Jennifer's voice, tiny and pathetic, sounding more like a girl half her age than her usual cocky self. I drew closer, curious and confused.

"I'm sorry, Daddy. I didn't want to do it, but Raven and the other girls started to make fun of me. They said I was immature, a baby, and I shouldn't be at parties yet."

"Don't you let them say those things about you, princess. Don't you even think it," I heard Uncle Reuben say.

If only he knew the whole truth, I thought, then what would he think of his little princess?

A moment later, Aunt Clara called for me. "Raven? Are you upstairs?" Uncle Reuben heard her call me and appeared in Jennifer's doorway.

"What are you doing up here?" he demanded.

"I came up to see Jennifer," I said.

"She's not well this morning, as you should know," he said. "Just tend to your chores."

"Daddy!" I heard her cry behind him.

"Go on!" he shouted at me.

I started down the stairs, turning to look up when I was almost halfway to the bottom. Jennifer's door was closed.

"What is it, dear?" Aunt Clara said.

I looked at her for a moment and thought about telling her about last night.

"It's nothing, Aunt Clara. I'll be right down." I wasn't ready to stoop to Jennifer's level. Not yet, at least.

Aunt Clara knew something was wrong, but she didn't press me for answers. I suppose she didn't want to know about Jennifer's behavior any more than she wanted to know about Uncle Reuben terrorizing William. Deep in her put-away heart, she couldn't be happy with the person Jennifer was becoming. She had to be aware of her deceitfulness, her laziness, and her meanness. I knew she was upset about the way William shut himself off from everyone, even her, and wanted the best for her son. So what about her daughter? What did she want for her?

And then I would reconsider and stop hating her and start pitying her. I had been here only a short time. I had no idea what sort of horrible things she had endured before I arrived. It was easy to see she was afraid of Uncle Reuben, maybe even more afraid of him than I was. All he had to do was raise his voice, lift his eyebrows, hoist his shoulders, and she would stammer and slink off, pressing her hands to her bosom and lowering her head. There were times when she didn't know I was looking at her, and I saw the deep sadness in her face or even caught her wiping a tear or two from her cheeks. Often, with her work done, she would sit in her rocking chair and rock with her eyes wide open, staring at nothing. She wouldn't even realize I was around.

I never doubted she loved her children, and maybe she once had loved Uncle Reuben, but she was someone who had been drained of her independence, her pride, and her strength, a hollow shadow of her former self who barely resembled the pretty young woman in the old pictures, a young woman with a face full of hope, whose future looked promising and wonderful, who had no reason to think that anything but roses and perfumed rain would fall around her.

Some adults, I thought, fall apart, drink, go to drugs, become wild and loose like my mother did when they lose their dreams. Some die a quiet sort of death, one hardly noticed, and live in the echo of other voices, their own real voices and smiles carried away in the wind like ribbons, gone forever, out of sight, visible only for a second or two in the glimmering eyes or soft smiles that come with the memories.

Late in the day, Jennifer emerged with that triumphant sneer on her face. I was dusting furniture after having vacuumed the living room. Uncle Reuben was taking a nap. William was in his room, and Aunt Clara had gone for groceries. Jennifer plopped on the sofa and put her feet up, shoes and all. I stopped and looked at her with disgust.

"I'm so tired," she said. "Lucky we didn't have school today."

"You got me in a lot of trouble," I said. "What stories did you spread around school about me? How could you tell so many filthy lies?"

"Your reputation preceded you," she said with a laugh. "I didn't have to spread any stories."

"You're really pitiful, Jennifer. You could at least tell your father the truth."

"Yeah, right. Then I'd be in trouble," she

said, and laughed. "You can keep cleaning. I won't be in your way. Just don't make too loud a noise."

"You're disgusting," I said, my anger boiling. "And in more ways than one."

"What's that supposed to mean?" she asked, making her eyes bigger. "You never drank too much, I suppose. In your house, it was probably a daily occurrence."

"For your information, it wasn't, at least for me." I stared at her a moment, debating whether or not I had the courage to say it. Finally, I did. "How could you let Brad do that to you? Don't you have any pride?"

She gazed at me, barely blinking. "What are you talking about now, Raven? What sort of lie are you trying to use to get out of trouble?" she asked.

"You know what I'm talking about, and you know it's not a lie," I said firmly.

Her expression didn't change. Then she looked away for a second before turning back to shake her head. "I don't know what you're talking about," she said, "and I'm warning you not to say anything that will make Daddy angry."

"He already got angry," I said. I put down the dust rag and undid my pants, lowering them and my panties. I turned to show her my welts.

"Ugh," she said, grimacing.

"He enjoyed doing it to me," I said, closing my pants. "He's a sadist, and he's perverted."

"Stop it!" She jumped off the sofa. "He's my father, and if he had to punish you, it was because you did something wrong. He's really kind, and he cares about me."

"You're just afraid of him. And you should be. If he knew how you really behaved, you'd get a far worse beating than I got," I said, drawing closer and staring into her face.

"Stop it!" she whispered. "He could hear you."

She stamped her foot on the floor. "What the hell's going on down there?" Uncle Reuben shouted from his bedroom.

Jennifer hesitated, staring at me with wide, scared eyes.

"Should I tell him?" I asked. "Should I tell him what really happened last night?"

She seemed to think, and then bet against me facing Uncle Reuben.

"Nothing, Daddy," she called back.

"Well, keep your voices down. I'm trying to get some rest. I didn't get much last night thanks to someone in this house," he added.

"Okay, Daddy. Raven's sorry," she said.

"You're sicker than he is," I said, shaking my head.

"You're just jealous because you don't have a father," she spit at me, her eyes narrow and hateful but also filling with tears. "You never had a father. You have a mother who is a tramp and a drug addict, and now you don't even have her," she said, gloating.

"No," I spit back at her, "but at least I still have some self-respect."

I threw down the dust rag and marched past her, practically knocking her out of my way.

"Who else would respect you?" she called after me. "You're worse than an orphan. You're nothing. You don't even have the right name! That's right, Daddy told me your mother was never even married, so don't go throwing stones. You're an illegitimate child!" she shouted.

I slammed the door closed behind me.

She was right, of course. Nothing she said wasn't true, but I'd rather be no one, I thought, than someone with a father like hers.

"Didn't I tell you two to shut up down there?" I heard Uncle Reuben scream.

"It's all right, Daddy. I'm taking a walk over to Paula's. If there's any more noise, it's not me making it," she shouted back. A moment later, I heard her leave the house, and it was all very quiet again.

I took a deep breath and went to the window. It was still gray and dismal outside. Jennifer had guessed correctly. I wouldn't tell Uncle Reuben. Why would he believe me? I'd keep her little secret. For now.

And then I saw someone on the corner standing under a sprawling maple tree. She wore a raincoat and a bandana over her hair just the way my mother often did.

"Mama?" I called, my eyes filling with tears.

The woman turned and disappeared down the next street.

I shot out of the room and rushed to the door. Then I ran down the walk and up the street to the corner, but by the time I got there, there was no one in sight. I stood there looking. Had I imagined it?

"Mama!" I screamed. My voice died in the wind, and no one appeared.

But what if it had been Mama? I thought. In my heart of hearts, I wished it had been, just so I knew she was thinking about me, just so I knew she did care a little, even if she hadn't come back for me.

Maybe, I thought, looking down the long, empty street with barely a car moving along it, maybe I wanted it so much that I simply imagined it.

Just like everything good I wanted for myself, this was only to be a dream, an illusion, another hope tied to a bubble that would burst, leaving me as lost and as forgotten as ever.

I turned and went back to the hell I had to call home.

8

Innocence Lost

The guidance counselor at my old school, Mr. Martin, once told me it's harder to look at yourself than it is to look at others. Some of my teachers had been complaining to him about me, and when I had my meeting with him and he read off the list of complaints, I had an excuse for everything. I was so good at dodging that he finally sat back, looked at me, and laughed.

"You don't believe half of what you're telling me, Raven," he said, "and you realize that when you walk out of here, you will walk out of here knowing that I don't believe you, either. The truth is, you have been irresponsible, neglectful, wasteful, and to a large extent self-destructive. You want to know what I think?" he asked, leaning forward and clasping his hands on the desk.

He had rust-colored hair and eyes as green as emeralds. Tiny freckles spilled from his forehead, down his temples to the crests of his cheeks. He always had a friendly hello for anyone. I never saw him lose his temper, but he had a way of making a troubled student feel bad about himself or herself. He spoke softly, sincerely, and acted as if he was everyone's big brother, taking each disappointment personally and asking questions that forced you to be honest.

My heart seemed to cower in my chest as I waited for him to drop his bombshell. I had to look down. His eyes were too penetrating, his gaze too demanding.

"No," I finally said, "but I guess you're going to tell me anyway."

"Yes, I am, Raven. I think you're a very angry young woman, angry about your life, and you think you're going to hurt someone if you do poorly and behave poorly. However, the only one you're really hurting is you."

I turned to look past him, to look out the office window, because I could feel the tears welling under my lids. Few people were ever able to penetrate the wall I had built around my true feelings, and whenever anyone did, I always felt a little naked and as helpless as a child.

142

"Your mother doesn't respond to any of my calls or letters. She's never been available to meet with your teachers."

"I don't care if she comes here or not," I snapped.

"Yes, you do," he said softly. He sat back again. "Sometimes, actually most of the time, we can't do much about the hand we've been dealt. We've got to make the most of it and get into the game. It doesn't do any good whining about it, right? You know that."

"I don't know what you're talking about, Mr. Martin. I failed some tests, big deal. My teachers are always picking on me because I'm an easy target. Other kids talk and pass notes and forget their books and stuff and don't get into half as much trouble."

Mr. Martin smiled. "When I was on the college basketball team and I gave my coach excuses like that, he would start to raise and lower his legs as if he were walking through a swamp," Mr. Martin said. "You know what I mean?"

I felt my throat close up and just shifted my eyes down.

"All right, Raven. I won't keep you any longer. You think over the things we discussed, and just know I'm here for you if you need to talk," he said.

I got up quickly, practically fleeing from his eyes and his probing questions. After I left his office, I stopped in the bathroom and looked at myself in the mirror. My eyes were red from the strain of holding back the tears. Mr. Martin was right: it was harder to look at myself, especially after he had held up a mirror of reality and truth.

Thinking back to that, I realized how much harder, if not impossible, it was for Jennifer to look at herself in a mirror. Everyone in my uncle's home suffered from the same self-imposed blindness, especially Aunt Clara, who not only turned away and kept her eyes down but also pretended she didn't know anything was wrong.

I left Mr. Martin's office feeling even more sorry for myself and a little guilty. Many of the students who behaved poorly or performed poorly left Mr. Martin's office angry at him for making them look into that mirror. I should have expected the same sort of behavior from Jennifer. After all, I had threatened to expose her to Uncle Reuben.

The rest of the weekend went as usual. I kept to myself, did my chores and my homework. Aunt Clara was always inviting me to join them in the living room to watch television, but the few times I had, I felt Uncle Reuben's eyes burning into me. When I glanced at him, he immediately looked disgusted or angry. He made me feel like a pebble in everyone's shoes. I felt as if I had to thank him for letting me breathe the very air in his house, and I knew that he would never give me anything willingly or with a full heart, not that I wanted anything from him. It hurt more that I had to depend on him for anything. This was truly what he called the burden of family relations, only it wasn't he who carried the weight of all that distress; it was me.

If I needed any reminders of the awkwardness between us, Jennifer was more than happy to provide them. She had ignored me most of the remainder of the weekend, but on Monday, as usual, she joined her friends at the bus stop, pretending I wasn't coming out of the same house with her. Our short-lived friendship to make it possible for her to attend the party was over. Ironically, because she had gotten herself sickly drunk and fooled around with Brad at Missy Taylor's, she was even more of a heroine to her friends. They were all waiting anxiously to hear the nitty-gritty details, as if throwing up your guts was a major accomplishment.

I sat in front with Clarence, but it was hard to ignore the raucous laughter coming from Jennifer and her clan in the rear. It wasn't until I was halfway through my morning that I began to understand why there were so many other students smiling at me, hiding their giggles, and wagging their heads. Just before lunch, some of them called out to me as they walked past Terri and me in the hallway.

"Heard you had a helluva weekend, Raven."

"Surprised you can walk."

"Who's next on your list?"

"Is it true what they say about girls with Latin blood?"

No one waited for a response. They just kept walking, their bursts of laughter trailing after them. The questions were tossed at me like cups of red paint meant to stain and ruin.

"What are they talking about?" Terri asked.

"I have no idea," I said. Afterward, when we sat in the cafeteria, I told her what had happened at Missy Taylor's party.

"So you rejected Mr. Wonderful," Terri said. "He's not going to let anyone know that."

"What do you mean?" I asked.

I saw Jimmy and Brad had joined Jennifer and her friends at a table, and they were all talking quickly and laughing. Once in a while, they turned to look at me. Someone made another remark, and they all roared. They sounded like a television laugh track. I felt the heat rise in my neck and into my face.

"I don't know what's going on," I said, "but it's coming to an end."

"What are you going to do?" Terri asked as I rose from my seat.

"Watch," I told her, and started to march across the cafeteria. I heard the laughter and chatter die down and saw that heads were turning my way. Everyone at Jimmy's table stopped talking and looked up.

"I hear that you're making up stories about me, Jimmy," I said, glaring down at him.

He shrugged. "Hey, in some cases, you don't have to make anything up," he said.

Jennifer grunted, and her friends smiled.

"In your case, I imagine it's ninety-five percent invented," I said. "After spending only a few minutes with you alone, I can understand why you're always looking for a new girl."

Smiles faded. I heard someone suck in air. Jimmy turned; his face was turning bright red. "And what's that supposed to mean?"

"You're a lot better at basketball than you

147

are at making love," I said. "I guess you waste all your talents on the court. If you don't stop making up nasty stories about me, I'll tell everyone why I left the bedroom so quickly."

For a moment, Jimmy was unable to respond. Everyone at the table turned from me to him, their eyes widening with new awareness. I knew there was no better way to make a boy like Jimmy afraid than to attack his manliness and his souped-up reputation.

"Huh?" was all he could utter.

I started to turn away when Jennifer piped up. "Stop trying to cover up, Raven. You're the one who's always fouling out," she shouted. "That's why you're here, living as a servant in my house." Her friends laughed.

I froze for a moment, feeling my spine turn to cold steel. Then I turned slowly and stepped back toward the table.

"Me? Cover up? Please, Daddy," I whimpered. "I didn't mean to throw up all over the place. Raven made me do it."

"Shut up!" she screamed.

"I'm a good girl. Daddy's little good girl," I mimicked.

Everyone held their breath. Jennifer turned so red I thought she might just burst into flames. Instead, she reached down, seized a half-eaten bowl of tomato soup, and threw it at me. The hot soup splattered my clothes and face, and the bowl crashed to the floor, shattering.

Mr. Wizenberg, the cafeteria monitor, came running over. "What's going on here?" he demanded. "Who did this?"

Everyone at the table stared at him. He turned to me. "Who threw that at you?"

"No one," I said. "It flew up on its own." I wouldn't be a tattletale, not even to get Jennifer in trouble.

Frustrated, Mr. Wizenberg sent the whole table and me to Mr. Moore's office. Unable to get anyone to rat, Mr. Moore put us all in detention and sent letters home to each and every student's family. Naturally, they all blamed me.

Before our letters arrived, Jennifer went crying to Uncle Reuben, claiming I had started it all. This time, Aunt Clara interceded before he could unbuckle his belt.

"Don't, Reuben," she said. "It can't be entirely her fault, and you've punished her enough already."

Uncle Reuben was angrier about Aunt Clara's interference than anything, but he didn't say a word. He pointed his finger at me and shook his hand without speaking.

To me, that was more frightening. He looked monstrous, capable of murder. I retreated as soon as I could and let him vent his rage to Aunt Clara.

"She is obviously the one who needs discipline, Clara. We can't keep her here if we don't try to control her bad ways. Look at all the trouble she's caused in the short time she's been with us. Don't ever interfere again, understand? Understand?" he threatened.

"Yes, Reuben, yes. I'll have a talk with her."

"Talking doesn't help that kind. She's too spoiled, too far gone. I'm her only hope," he declared.

If he was my only hope, I was long gone.

When the letter arrived, he pinned mine on the inside of my bedroom door.

"Don't you dare take this off here, understand?" he declared. "I want you to see this each and every time you walk out of this room."

"Are you pinning Jennifer's to her door, too?" I asked.

"Don't you worry about Jennifer. You worry about yourself. That's enough," he snapped.

I couldn't keep the emotion from my face, and I saw him tilt his head as he looked at me, his own eyes focusing like tiny micro-scopes to look into my thoughts.

"You might have Clara fooled with that sweet act you put on," he said in a hard, coarse whisper, "but I know your mother. I knew your father. I know from where you come. You can't fool me."

"If my mother was so bad, why aren't you? You're her brother. You came from the same parents. You grew up together, didn't you? You're not perfect," I said. "You've done some bad things." The moment I said that, I knew I had gone too far, but I had no idea just how far.

He stepped farther into the room.

"What did she tell you?" he asked. "Did she make up some lie about me? Spit it out. Spit out the garbage. Go on," he ordered.

I shook my head. "There's nothing to tell," I said, my heart pounding. He seemed to expand, inflate, rise higher, and grow wider.

"I never did anything to her," he said. "If I ever hear you say anything, I swear I'll tear out your tongue."

I stared at him, and then I looked down quickly. He hovered there like a giant cat. I could almost feel my bones crumbling under his pounce.

"She was disgusting, parading around

naked and saying whatever she wanted, trying to get me to give in to her evil ways. Well, I showed her. It was good when she ran off, only she didn't run far enough," he declared.

I could almost feel his hot breath on the top of my head, but I didn't move, didn't twitch a muscle. I tried to stop breathing, to close my eyes and pretend I was somewhere else. After what seemed like an eternity, he turned and marched out. It felt as if a cold draft had followed him and left me in a vacuum of horribly dark silence. I was afraid to think, even to imagine what sort of things he meant.

Suddenly, I felt I had to get fresh air. I threw on a sweater and went out. All the houses on the street and the next were well spaced apart. There were only about six or seven on each avenue. At the moment, there was no one on the street and apparently no one outside his or her home. I folded my arms under my breasts and walked with my head down, not really paying attention to where I was going. I was so deep in thought that I never realized I had crossed the street.

"Hey," I heard, and looked up at Clarence Dunsen. "Wh . . . where are you . . . you going?"

He had a garbage bag in his hand and had

just lifted the lid of the can when he saw me.

I stopped and looked around, surprised at how far I had traveled.

"I'm just taking a walk," I said.

He put the garbage in the can and closed it. Then he simply stood there looking at me.

"Is this where you live?" I asked, nodding at the modest ranch-style home. It had gray siding with charcoal shutters, a large lawn with some hedges around the walk, and a red maple tree in front. The garage door was open, and a station wagon and a pickup truck were visible. I saw a bike hanging on the wall as well and what looked like some tools, wrenches and pliers, clipped to another wall.

"Yeah," he said. "I live in the bas . . . bas . . . basement."

"The basement?" I smiled. "What do you mean?"

"That's where I . . . slee . . . sleep and stuff," he replied. He smiled. "I have my own door."

I shook my head, still confused.

"Com . . . come on. I'll shhh . . . show you," he urged with a gesture. He took a few steps toward the side of the house and waited. I thought a moment, looked around the empty street, and then followed him to steps that led down to a basement door. He pointed. "There," he said.

"You live down there?"

"A-huh. Wanna sssssss . . . see?"

No one had ever told me about this, not even Jennifer, but then again, no one really took any interest in Clarence except to make fun of his stuttering. I nodded again and followed him down the steps. He opened the door to a small bedroom that contained a desk and chair, a dresser, a cabinet that served as a closet, and a small table on top of which sat a television set. The floor was covered in a dark brown linoleum with a small gray oval rug at the foot of the bed. Under the bed were a few pairs of shoes and some sneakers. There were two electric heaters along the sides of the room.

His clothing was tossed about, shirts over the chair, a pair of pants dangling over the door of the closet, and some T-shirts folded and left on top of the television set. I saw magazines on the floor, some books, and a few boxes of puzzles.

"Why do you have to live down here?" I asked him. The room had no windows and was lit by a ceiling fixture and one standing lamp beside the desk.

"My mom's new hus . . . husband fixed it for . . . for me so the baby could have my old rooo . . . room," he said.

The dull gray cement walls had chips and cracks in them. It smelled dank and musty. The floor rafters were clearly visible above us, and there were cobwebs in them. This was more like a dungeon than a bedroom, I thought. Why would his mother want him down here? I could hear footsteps above us, the sound of chair legs scratching the floor, and then a baby's wail.

"That's Donna Marie," he said.

I nodded and continued to look around the dingy room. "Where is your bathroom?"

"Upsta . . . stairs. You got to go?"

"No," I said, smiling. "I just wondered. You do puzzles?" I asked, nodding at the boxes on the floor.

"Yeah, sometimes. Aft . . . after I do one, I take, take, take it apart and do it again."

I laughed, and he smiled.

Just then, the door of his room was pulled open, and a tall, lean, dark-haired man in a pale white athletic undershirt, jeans, and old slippers appeared. He was unshaven and had a square jaw with a cleft chin and a thin nose under a pair of dark brown, tired eyes that brightened with interest when he saw me.

"Who the hell are you?" he asked.

"I'm Raven Flores."

"Who's this, Clarence?" He smiled. "A girlfriend?"

"Nnnnn . . . no," Clarence replied, turning a deep red. He glanced at me with terror.

"I'm just a neighbor," I said. "I'm living with my uncle."

"Who's that?"

"Reuben Stack."

His smile widened. "Reuben, huh? He never mentioned you. I work with him." He turned back to Clarence. "We was wondering why you didn't come back upstairs after you took out the garbage. It's time for dinner. I hate to interrupt," he said, smiling at me. "Come on back later, if you want."

"That's all right. I'll see you tomorrow, Clarence," I said.

"Sure you're not coming back tonight?" his stepfather asked. I ignored him and went to the door. His laughter followed me out.

I hurried back, feeling sorrier for Clarence than I did for myself. Where was this magical family in America, the one I saw on television? You can have parents and still be an orphan, I thought.

"Where the hell have you been?" Uncle Reuben asked when I entered the house.

"I just went for a walk."

"It's suppertime. You know you have to

156

be here to help," he said.

I hurried toward the kitchen.

"Jennifer's already set the table," he said.

"All by herself?" I retorted.

"Don't get smart," he snapped. "Just help Clara bring in the food, and next time, you let someone know when you're leaving the house, hear?"

"Yes, sir," I said. I nearly saluted.

He stared daggers at me, so I continued into the kitchen, where Aunt Clara was busy getting the food into serving bowls. She worked quickly and quietly. I had the feeling Uncle Reuben had already blamed her for my not being there.

"I'm sorry I'm late, Aunt Clara, but . . ."

"Just take this in, dear," she said, handing me the bowl of mashed potatoes.

When I entered the dining room, I found Jennifer sitting back with a wide, self-satisfied smile on her face. William looked as meek and beaten down as ever, and Uncle Reuben sat in his throne, his big arms on the table, waiting like the king he thought he was.

"It's about time," Jennifer said. "I'm starving. I got the table set for you."

I put down the bowl and looked at the plates and silverware.

"Forks are on the wrong side," I said, and

157

winked at William, who gave me a small smile. Then I returned to the kitchen before Jennifer could offer a smart reply.

It was another dinner with Uncle Reuben pronouncing his opinions about women and young people. The world was out of control. Values were being destroyed, and the fabric of the country was being torn apart. It was all the fault of women who wanted too much and children who weren't disciplined properly. No one contradicted him. I tried to drown him out with my own thoughts, but he bellowed and knocked on the table when he wanted to force home his conclusions.

All Aunt Clara could say was, "Don't excite yourself when you're eating, Reuben."

I hurried to clean up afterward. As usual, Jennifer just rose and went upstairs, not even bringing her own plate to the sink. I saw that William wanted to help, but he was afraid of angering his father, who had just finished declaring that women were getting men to do their work and that was one of the things wrong with this country.

After my chores, I went to my room to start my homework. I could hear Jennifer in the living room watching television with Uncle Reuben and Aunt Clara. Her laughter sounded loud and obnoxious to me. Why didn't they ask her about her schoolwork? I wondered. I heard the phone ring, and a few minutes later, my door was thrust open.

Uncle Reuben stood there gaping in at me.

"What?" I asked, turning from my small table.

"Where'd you go before?" he asked, stepping into the room and closing the door behind him. "Huh?"

"I told you. I went for a walk," I said.

"That's a lie. You went to the Dunsen house, didn't you?"

"I saw Clarence, and he wanted to show me his room in the basement," I said.

Uncle Reuben smiled coldly and shook his head. "You know that boy's retarded."

"He's not retarded. He just has a speech problem," I said.

"It's easier to take advantage of someone like that. What were you trying to do, seduce him?"

"No!" I cried. "Leave me alone."

"I got to get a call from one of the men who works under me gloating that he caught you with his stepson? I got to get that call? What are you doing to our reputation in the neighborhood?"

I turned away, the tears coming so fast

and hard I couldn't stop them this time. I wasn't the one who was fooling around with boys, and yet I was getting accused!

"Looks like you need more than one lesson, and more than one lesson you're going to get," he said, and pulled off his belt. "Get on that bed."

"No. Leave me alone!" I cried.

"If you get on it yourself, I'll only give you six whacks. If you make me do it, it's ten," he said. He hovered between me and the door. I could never get around him. "Well? Which will it be?"

"I didn't do anything wrong," I moaned. "Please."

"Looks like ten," he said, moving toward me.

"No," I cried, holding up my hands. I got up and backed toward the bed.

"Reuben, what's going on in there?" I heard Aunt Clara ask.

"Just keep out of this, Clara, or it will go down harder for everyone," he shouted. He turned to me. I couldn't stop sobbing. I didn't want to be hit once, much less ten times. What could I do?

I went to the bed.

"Lower 'em," he ordered.

Sobbing harder, I reached under my skirt and lowered my panties. He pushed me forward and once again held me down as he whacked me six times with the belt.

"You don't go to any boy's room alone," he said. "And stay away from that retard, hear?"

I couldn't talk. I bit down on the blanket and waited. I felt him run his palm over my rear, and then I heard him march to the door and leave, closing it behind him. It took me a while to catch my breath and pull up my panties. I lay back in the bed and cursed him over and over, praying he would fall down the stairs and break his neck. I fantasized standing over his corpse, spitting on it, kicking it. I didn't think it was possible to hate anyone as much as I hated him.

My door opened again, and I turned in terror. It was Jennifer. She stood there shaking her head.

"Clarence Dunsen? You walked out on Jimmy Freer and went to Clarence Dunsen?"

"No," I said.

She smiled and shook her head. "Wait until everyone hears about this. If I were you, I would crawl under that bed and stay there," she advised, and walked away, laughing.

I lay there, my body like an empty glass filling with red liquid hate. Nearly two hours later, I heard them all go upstairs to sleep. I waited a little longer, and then I went to the door, my hands clenched in fists, my chest so tight my heart had trouble beating. Quietly but determined, I marched up the stairs. It was dark and still. Uncle Reuben and Aunt Clara's door was shut, as were William's and Jennifer's. I could hear Jennifer talking softly on her telephone and then laughing.

I opened the door, and she looked up from the floor where she was curled.

"What do you want?" she demanded.

"If you spread that story about me," I said, "I will tell your father what really happened the night of Missy's party."

I closed the door and walked down the stairs, somehow forgetting and ignoring the pain from my belt beating.

9

I'm Not Going to Take It

Jennifer was so quiet the next morning, she made me nervous at breakfast. She wouldn't look at me, and if she did have to gaze my way, it was as if she was looking right through me. She looked tired, her eyes dark. I imagined she had been sleeping on my threat, and it had played like a pebble under the sheet, causing her to toss and turn, flitting through her nightmares.

My hands fluttered around so that I nearly dropped a dish. Uncle Reuben was poised to pounce if I did. He kept looking at me with sparks in his eyes when I rattled cups and saucers. Jennifer kept her eyes down. Every once in a while, she would lift her chin, and I saw her puckered little prune mouth drawn up like a drawstring purse. She ate and gathered her things together with barely a syllable escaping from those tight lips.

"Are you feeling all right, Jennifer?" Aunt Clara finally asked her. I wasn't the only one who noticed a marked difference in her behavior. Usually, she didn't shut up, blabbing like someone who loved the sound of her own voice and expected everyone else to adore it as well.

Jennifer stabbed me with her nasty glare immediately after Aunt Clara's question. I half expected her to burst out with new accusations, revealing my threat. I braced myself in anticipation.

"I'm fine," she said. "I'm just tired."

"I hope you're not coming down with anything," Aunt Clara said.

Uncle Reuben's eyebrows jerked upward as if pulled by strings. "Everyone's been healthy in this house up until now," he muttered.

Did he really see me as some sort of walking, talking germ, a carrier of disease and illness, someone full of infection and decay?

"Maybe you should stay home today," Aunt Clara suggested.

"Oh, no," Jennifer said with a deep and

painful sigh, "I have tests to take, and I just can't afford to miss any work."

Please spare me, I wanted to say. Since when did she care one iota about her work? She either cheated or borrowed other people's homework, and if she could find a way to get out of a test, she wouldn't hesitate. Suddenly, poor Jennifer was going to be the martyr? Now I did think what I ate would come back up. I rose from the table, clearing off dirty dishes.

Jennifer was out of the house ahead of me as usual. With the chores I had to complete — helping with the breakfast dishes, cleaning the table, organizing and fixing my little room — I nearly missed the bus. Aunt Clara hurried me along, and I charged out of the house, running down the sidewalk just as the last student boarded. As usual, there was an empty seat next to Clarence. He looked up timidly, and I smiled and sat beside him. Jennifer was in the rear with her friends.

"I'm sor . . . sorry about my . . . my . . . stepfa . . . fa . . . father," Clarence said. "He's a jerk."

"It's all right, Clarence. Don't worry about it. I didn't think much of him," I said.

"He's got a nas . . . nasty mind. He made a lot of jokes after," Clarence said.

165

"Where's your real father?" I asked.

He shrugged. "I don't know. Maybe he's in California. I can't hardly remem . . . remem . . . ber him anymore," he said sadly, and looked out the bus window.

There was a slight drizzle, the drops flattening against the glass and then spreading out wider to form what looked like spider webs. Gray skies made the morning seem more dismal than usual. Everyone on the bus was subdued. The conversations were quiet, and there was little laughter. When I gazed back, I saw Jennifer glaring my way, holding her books and bouncing with the bus. Even her normally buoyant and noisy friends looked half asleep.

The school became darker and darker inside as the clouds thickened outside. Some of the corridors weren't as well lit as others, and it felt as if I were moving through tunnels to get to my classes this particular morning. As the rain grew stronger and pounded in sheets against the school walls and windows, students grew sleepy. Even the teachers seemed to struggle with enthusiasm for the work.

Just before lunch, however, the rain stopped, and a bit of sunshine broke through. It washed away the drowsiness, and voices grew louder. Students walked faster, teased and joked with each other.

At lunchtime, Terri and I headed for the cafeteria, talking about an upcoming movie. I used to go to the movies once in a while when I lived with my mother, but now I didn't know when I would get to go again.

Suddenly, we heard a burst of loud laughter from a corner of the corridor. At least a dozen or so boys were gathered in a huddle. When they turned, I saw that Jimmy was there. I stiffened instinctively, but as the boys continued to separate, I discovered they had been surrounding poor Clarence Dunsen. He looked terrified.

"Here she . . . she . . . come . . . comes, Clarence," Jimmy said. "Why don't you tell her how much you la . . . la . . . love her," he shouted, and all the boys laughed.

"Leave him alone," I ordered.

"We're not bothering him. Clarence was just telling us about your rendezvous in his bedroom the other day," Jimmy said loudly enough for everyone around us to hear.

"You bastard," I told him, which only made him and the boys laugh harder.

I hurried into the cafeteria, Terri trailing quickly behind.

"What's that all about?" she asked.

"My cousin has been at it again," I said,

fuming. I threw my books on the table and folded my arms.

"Don't do anything violent," Terri advised. She nodded toward Mr. Wizenberg, who was watching me like a nervous rabbit. I searched for Jennifer and found her holding court at a table across the cafeteria. She looked so self-satisfied, I felt like ripping out her eyes.

The boys erupted into the cafeteria behind Clarence, who tried to get to his usual table. They were chanting behind him.

"I la . . . la . . . la . . . love you, Ray . . . Ray . . . Raven."

The whole cafeteria turned, and Clarence, who was bright red, dropped to his seat and stared down at the tabletop.

"Quiet!" Mr. Wizenberg shouted. "I said *quiet!*"

The boys stopped and spread out to their tables, laughing and congratulating themselves with pats on their backs. Jimmy went to Jennifer, and they had a good laugh together.

"What's going on?" Terri asked.

I told her what had happened, but I didn't say anything about telling Uncle Reuben about Jennifer and Brad. I couldn't get myself to fall to Jennifer's level. Maybe she had known that all the while. When she rose to go to the lunch line, I jumped up.

Terri seized my forearm. "Careful," she warned. "You'll get suspended this time for sure."

I nodded but charged forward. "You're a horrible person, Jennifer," I said, pushing my way behind her. "Don't you care who you hurt?"

"I don't know what you're talking about. I didn't tell anyone anything," she said, flipping her hair back. "Clarence bragged about you and him to a couple of his friends, and it got out."

"That's a lie. You're such a liar." I stepped closer to her, and she backed away.

"If you cause any more trouble, Daddy will put you in the street," she warned.

"I'd rather be in the street. There's less dirt."

A surge of panic ran through her eyes as she looked around to see if anyone was really listening to us.

"Don't you dare say anything terrible about me or my family, Raven. Don't you dare," she said in a weak whisper.

"You're so disgusting," I said, shaking my head. Some of the girls did pause to listen. I hesitated.

"Don't worry," I said. "I won't get down in the mud with you."

She smiled, crooked and mean.

I left her and returned to my table, frustrated, raging, my anger simmering my blood into a rolling boil.

"Easy," Terri said, putting her hand on my arm and nodding toward the rear. Mr. Wizenberg had come up right behind me. He rocked on his heels a moment with his hands behind his back, and then he glared a stern warning at me as he continued across the cafeteria.

"Everyone thinks I'm the cause of trouble here," I moaned. "It's not fair."

"She'll get hers," Terri predicted. "Someday."

For now, that had to be how I would leave it. I went to my classes after lunch, the rest of the day moving more quickly. I was relieved when the last bell rang and we headed for the buses to go home. This time, when I boarded the bus, I hesitated. I knew if I sat with Clarence, Jennifer and her friends would make more fun of him. It was for his benefit that I passed him by. He looked up at me with sad eyes. I tried to smile to indicate it was better I didn't sit next to him today. He seemed to understand, and I moved deeper into the bus, finding an empty seat. No one sat beside me.

We started for home. At first, there was

just the usual sound of chatter and hilarity, but suddenly, there was a shrill laugh I recognized as Jennifer's. I turned just as she and her friends began their chanting.

"I la . . . la . . . la . . . love you, Ray . . . Ray . . . Raven."

A sea of laughter swept over the bus. Everyone was smiling, and soon everyone was into the chant. The bus driver looked confused, a silly smile on her lips. She was a stout woman named Peggy Morris with hair chopped short about her ears. She wore flannel shirts and jeans and had the sleeves of her shirt rolled to the elbows. Despite her tough appearance, I always found her pleasant and friendly.

I looked at Clarence. He slapped his hands over his ears and rocked in his seat.

"Stop it!" I shouted, which only brought more laughter. "You idiots. Stop!"

They chanted louder. I was hoping Peggy Morris would do something, but she was too involved with a car that was slowing and speeding erratically in front of us.

Suddenly, Clarence shot up from his seat and screamed like a wounded animal. His voice reverberated through the bus, but instead of bringing the chanting to a halt, it drew more laughter and then louder chanting. Clarence covered his ears. I was yelling for them to stop, too. It all sounded like bedlam, like a bus filled with insane people. Peggy had just started to turn, slowing the bus down, when Clarence surprised everyone by deliberately smashing his fist against the window. The first slam brought the chanting to a halt. I could barely utter a sound, my throat choking up.

"Clarence!" I managed, but he did it again, harder this time, and the glass shattered.

He stood there, the blood streaming down the side of his arm. Girls screamed. Even some of the boys cried out. Peggy Morris jammed her foot on the brakes and pulled the bus to the side just as Clarence fell backward. She caught him before he rolled over the railing and onto the bus steps.

Everyone grew deadly quiet. I made my way down the aisle. Peggy shouted for me to hand her the first aid kit, and I hurried to do so. She opened it and pressed a fistful of gauze against Clarence's hand and arm. Then she looked up at me.

"Go out and get to a phone," she said. "Call for an ambulance. Quickly!"

When she opened the door, I shot down the steps and into a convenience store on the corner. The man behind the counter called 911 for me, and I returned to the bus. Everyone remained subdued, even Jennifer. The driver did the best she could to stem the flow of blood. Clarence lay there with his eyes closed. What seemed like an hour but was only minutes passed before we heard the sound of an ambulance followed by a police car. Chatter began again as the paramedics boarded the bus quickly, heard what had happened, and tended to Clarence. Moments later, they were carrying him off the bus on a stretcher. As soon as he was placed in the ambulance, Peggy Morris returned and stood with her hands on her wide hips, glaring angrily at everyone, her face still pale from the shock and excitement.

"I don't want to hear another peep," she said shakily. "Not another peep."

She started up the bus, and we rode to our stops in funereal silence. My heart was thumping. I had a revolting nausea whirling in my stomach. When our stop appeared, I rose and walked slowly down the steps.

"Thanks for your help," Peggy Morris said. I nodded and got off.

As I started up the sidewalk, Jennifer whipped past me, pausing only to say, "You have only yourself to blame."

It took every ounce of restraint to keep

from rushing up behind her to seize the back of her hair and pull out every strand as I kicked and pummeled her sneering, ugly face. But I knew I could never sink to her level, no matter what. I would never be that evil.

Uncle Reuben knew about Clarence before he came home that night. Clarence's stepfather had been called at work and had to rush over to the hospital. Uncle Reuben didn't know any of the details, but I saw from the way he looked at me when he asked questions that he assumed I had something to do with it.

"What happened?" he began.

"Clarence went nuts," Jennifer said.

"Why?"

"The kids were teasing him, and he went nuts. He's nuts anyway," she said.

"What do you mean, they were teasing him? How were they teasing him?"

"Making fun of his stuttering," she said.

"That's all?" he followed, still eyeing me suspiciously.

"I don't know, Daddy. I wasn't paying attention. Suddenly, he smashed his hand into the window. Now, isn't that nuts?" she cried.

"How horrible," Aunt Clara said.

"Was he bleeding?" William asked.

"A lot. That's why they had to get the ambulance," Jennifer told him. William grimaced and looked to me.

"Mighty strange how all these terrible things are suddenly happening," Uncle Reuben declared.

Afterward, Jennifer had the nerve to come to tell me she had done me a favor. "I protected you," she said, "so don't go blaming me for anything."

"How did you protect me?" I said, amazed at her boldness.

"I didn't tell Daddy why Clarence was being teased. He'd be real mad then, so you just better be nice to me, or . . ."

I shook my head. "I'd rather be nice to a rattlesnake," I told her. "You and Uncle Reuben deserve each other."

"I'll tell him you said that," she threatened. "You want another beating?"

"Leave me alone."

"I need some of my blouses ironed, and I don't have the time," she said. "I'll send them down with William, and you better not damage them, or else."

Later that evening, I heard Uncle Reuben tell Aunt Clara that Clarence's stepfather had called. He said Clarence had to have twenty stitches and was being kept in the hospital for observation. He said he might even have to go to the psychiatric ward.

"I don't know how yet," he concluded, "but I'm sure Raven had something to do with this."

"Oh, Reuben, no. She wouldn't," Aunt Clara assured him.

"I'll find out. Trouble, that's all she is, trouble just waiting to happen. Damn my sister. She should have been sterilized."

What a horrible thing to say, I thought, but I did feel just terrible about Clarence. In a strange sort of way, I supposed I was responsible. If I hadn't let him talk me into showing me his basement room, the kids wouldn't have made up the chant. I bring disaster to everyone I touch, I thought. Uncle Reuben isn't so wrong.

Clarence's self-inflicted wound and the entire event on the bus were the big topic of discussion at school the next day. The kids who had tormented him didn't feel any remorse. If anything, they behaved as if they had helped bring out his mental illness. Now he would be where he belonged . . . in a nut house. They were so smug I couldn't stand it. Clarence did not return, and in my way of thinking, he was the one who was better off.

Later that week, Clarence's stepfather

somehow found out about the subject of the chanting and teasing, and he told Uncle Reuben. When he came home, armed with the knowledge, he wore a look of self-satisfaction on his face. He proudly announced to Aunt Clara that I was indeed the cause of the trouble. For the time being, he seemed content being proven right. Aunt Clara retreated even more deeply into her shell, and Uncle Reuben's tyranny raged unchecked. He was what he wanted to be, king of his own home, supreme judge and jury, and we existed only for his pleasure and comfort.

My chores were increased. I wasn't permitted to go anywhere with anyone on the weekends for at least a month. No after-school activities, parties, not even a trip to the shopping mall. Aunt Clara put up little or no argument. A cloud fell over the house, even more dark and oppressive than the ones that had preceded it.

I waited and hoped for news of my mother. Nothing came. All Uncle Reuben would say was that she was on everyone's most wanted list.

"Why should she show her face around here?" he declared with a cold laugh. "She's got a brother assuming her responsibilities."

My mother had done many cruel and

stupid things to me, but the worst, I thought, was leaving me with her brother.

I couldn't imagine how things could get worse.

But they could.

And they did.

10

Home Alone

Being confined to the house while everyone else was out doing things on the weekend wasn't actually all that bad. I would have enjoyed it even more if William, who seemed to enjoy my company more than he did anyone else's in the family, had been able to stay home, too. However, Aunt Clara took him to the mall to buy him new clothes and a new pair of sneakers Saturday afternoon. Jennifer went to a matinee with her friends. Before she left, she stopped to gloat by the sewing room, where I was ironing clothes.

"Everyone's meeting for pizza, and then we're going to the movies. I'm sitting with Brad," she bragged, "so no matter what you think, he really is interested in me."

"I'm happy for you," I said dryly.

"If you weren't so mean to me, I might get

the kids to like you, too," she offered.

"Me? Mean to you?" I smiled. "Do you really believe that, or do you think I'm that stupid?"

"I think you're that stupid," she said, pulling her thick lower lip into her cheek.

"You know," I said, spinning around on her, "I came here feeling sorry for myself and even envying you. You have parents, a nice house, a very nice little brother. You seemed to have everything I ever wanted, and then I got to know you better and see what really goes on here, and now you know what?"

"What?"

"I feel sorrier for you than I do for myself," I said, and turned back to my ironing.

"I have no idea what you're talking about. You're nuts, just like Clarence. I don't know why I even bothered trying to be your friend," she snapped.

"Becoming your friend is like becoming friends with a black widow spider," I retorted.

She spun on her heels and charged out the front door, slamming it so hard the whole house shook and the windows rattled. I smiled to myself, turned on the radio, and started to enjoy my solitude. Uncle Reuben had already left to bowl with his team.

There were so few times when I had a chance to be alone and not feel I was being watched or judged.

I had to face the fact that my mother would never come for me or be able to take me to live with her again. When she was caught, they would put her in a real jail this time, and even if she behaved and was released, she would probably be released to another drug rehabilitation clinic. After that, she still might not be allowed to have me live with her, and who knew if she would even want the responsibility?

Perhaps I should stop fighting reality, I thought. I was only hurting myself. I was like someone bound with piano wire, struggling and squirming to be free and only tearing myself to pieces. I had to learn to ignore, to look the other way, to pretend, to make up my own world. Maybe Aunt Clara wasn't all wrong behaving as she did. At least she found some peace in her life by deliberately blinding herself to the unpleasantness in her family. She was able to go on, to face every new morning with fresh hope.

I was really like someone caught in a strong current being carried downstream. I could struggle and struggle, desperately try to fight the water and only waste my strength, or I could turn in the direction the water was flowing and try to swim a little faster than the current. Maybe, if I stayed even a few inches ahead of my fate, I would feel some sense of purpose, some meaning and identity, and be able to think of myself as real, a person with a name, with some control over what would happen to her. The current couldn't go on forever and ever. It would take me someplace, drop me at some shore, and if I endured and stayed strong, I would be able to stand on my own two feet and then, then, make a new life for myself.

That was the only hope I had, the only choice left. Realizing it was like lifting a weight from my shoulders. I actually began to feel good and swayed my body to the music as I worked. I sang along with the singers. I went to the kitchen and poured myself a soda and returned to my room to finish the ironing. After that, I thought I would take a shower and just spend the rest of the day reading, catching up with my English assignments.

It was turning out to be one of the nicest days I had spent living with my uncle and aunt. I laughed to myself realizing that the reason it was so nice was that no one else was home. I washed my hair in the shower and then sat before the small mirror in my room and dried my hair, first with a towel and then with Aunt Clara's blow dryer. My hair was truly my crowning glory, long and thick. My mother always coveted my hair, moaning about her own thin, split strands and then running her fingers through my hair and bringing it to hers as if touching mine might transfer some of the richness to her own.

I sat there in the blue cotton robe Aunt Clara had given me and fantasized, dreaming myself into scenarios with a handsome young man who would come along and see me for myself, fall in love with me, and sweep me away from all this. Why couldn't I be a real Cinderella? Somewhere out there surely was a young man destined to be my lover, my husband, my prince, a young man who would see my strengths as well as my beauty and want me at his side forever and ever.

I was in such a reverie, actually hearing the music, the voices, feeling the wind in my hair as we drove along picturesque country roads, laughing, kissing, and promising our love to each other, that I never heard Uncle Reuben come into the house, nor did I hear him come into my room. It wasn't until he was actually standing behind me, swaying, his eyes glassy, that I realized he was there. I spun around on my chair and looked up at him.

"Getting yourself all dolled up for someone else, are you?" he asked with a cold, crooked smile on his face.

"No. I did all my chores and just wanted to clean up and do my homework," I said. I couldn't believe how timid I sounded. I was wrapped so tightly inside my heart could barely beat.

"Get clean? You?" He shook his head and snorted. "You're dirty through and through," he said. "All the soap and hot water in the world couldn't clean you up."

"That's not so. I'm not dirty!" I insisted.

"You're your mother's daughter. You've proven that in just the short time you've been here," he responded. "Seducing that retarded boy," he muttered.

"I didn't do that."

"Go on with you," he said, waving his hand. "You'll never change. It's just bad blood."

"If there's bad blood in this family," I said, making my eyes small, "it's more in you than in my mother and me."

He stepped back and blinked as if I had reached up and slapped his face.

"Z'at so?" he said. "You still have a big mouth, eh?" He wobbled as he stared down at me. I could smell beer on his breath. It churned my stomach. "I oughtta just throw you out or turn you over to the court and let them put you in one of them orphanages."

"I wish you would. Then I would tell everyone how awful you are — how you terrorize your family with threats and beatings," I blurted.

This time, his eyes widened, and he opened and shut his mouth without a sound. He wobbled, and then his face reddened.

"What are you talking about? What kind of filthy lies have you been spreading? Who did you tell such stories?"

"Nobody," I said. "Yet."

Despite his unsteady stance and his dull, dizzy look, he managed to bring his hand around so quickly and accurately that he struck me across the cheek before I had a chance to lift my arm to protect myself. The blow stung, and the force of it drove me off the seat. I fell to one knee. Before I could turn to stand, he had the back of my robe up as he pulled me closer.

"Naked? Naked sitting here?" he cried.

"It's supposed to be my room," I wailed.

"With the door wide open? You're a tart, a tease, just like your mother was. I'll have to teach you the same lesson I taught her. I'll show you what happens to girls like you."

He reached down and seized me at the

waist, lifting me as if I weighed nothing and dropping me on the bed.

"*No!*" I screamed. "Don't touch me!"

He slapped me sharply across my buttocks and then sat beside me as he pulled my robe up farther until it was at my waist.

"That's all you do want is to be touched," he said, suddenly in a softer voice. Nevertheless, that frightened me more. I felt an icy chill travel up my spine, and I turned to get away, but he rested his heavy torso against my ribs and back, and I was pinned beneath him.

I felt his hand on my rear end again and then down between my thighs.

"Just like your mother, all you want is to be touched," he said. I jumped and screamed when his fingers traveled to where I hesitated even to touch myself. "You're bringing shame into my home," he muttered as he continued.

Then, as if he had suddenly realized what he was doing, he stopped and slapped me again.

"Everyone at the bowling alley was talking about the Dunsen boy and what you done. It was embarrassing. They wanted to know what sort of niece I had living with me. You don't listen. You keep being bad," he said. "I've been too easy on you."

He leaned forward and found my hairbrush. The first blow stung so badly I really did see stars. Lights flashed in my eyes. The pain spread out along my back and sides as if I were a plate of glass, shattering. He hit me again and again; his aim was off so that some of the blows fell on my thighs, each taking the breath out of me. When he was finished, he remained on the couch, breathing hard over me.

"You'll get worse if you do another bad thing. I'll burn the skin off you, understand?"

He pinched the flesh under my buttocks harder and harder. "Understand?"

"Yes," I cried. "Yes."

"Good. Good," he said, rising. "Don't you go crying to Clara about this, either, understand? If you do . . ."

I didn't move until I heard him stumble out of the room, closing the door behind him. When I did move, I couldn't believe the burning and the pain. It was the worst beating of all and the most degrading.

I groaned, turned over on my back, and lay there staring up at the ceiling. It was how Aunt Clara found me later. She thought I was sick, and I told her I was just having a bad time with my period. She believed that and let me be, offering to do all the preparation for dinner. As if he wanted to play along, Uncle Reuben did not challenge my story. Jennifer couldn't care less and never even poked her head in to tell me how much of a good time she had had with her friends. William looked in on me, and I tried desperately to hide my pain and agony from him, but he seemed to sense it anyway. His eyes were full of suspicion and fear.

Later, when I came out of my room to join them at supper, I did walk like a girl who was suffering menstrual cramps. Aunt Clara talked about how terrible it was that modern medicine could find cures for almost everything but that.

"Maybe that's because most doctors are men," she muttered.

"That's nonsense, women's lib propaganda," Uncle Reuben piped in, and then went into one of his tirades about the standards in our society crumbling with all the liberal movements in politics and government.

I went to bed early and spent most of the next day in my room lying in bed. The pain went so deeply this time that it changed from a stinging to an aching. I ate little and slept as much as I could. The next morning, Monday, Uncle Reuben did order me to get up and help with the morning chores.

"And don't try to stay home from school, either," he warned. "I know you did a lot of that when you lived with my sister. She probably lost track of the days," he added.

Walking was still painful, but I was terrified that he would think of another excuse to hit me if I didn't obey him. I boarded the bus and rode silently to school. During my morning classes, I had to fidget and squirm a great deal to find comfortable, less painful positions. Only Mr. Gatlin noticed and asked if I had ants in my pants. That drew laughter and more whispering and teasing in the halls between classes.

My real problem was in gym class. I tried using my period as an excuse, but Mrs. Wilson wanted me to suit up anyway and stand at the sidelines. I pleaded, but she was insistent.

"My girls always suit up," she claimed. "Those are my rules. No loafers here," she added. She watched me leave her office, and minutes later, while I was changing, she came into the locker room and spied on me.

"My God," she cried, "what happened to you?"

I spun around, holding my uniform to my chest. The welts and black-and-blue marks on my upper thighs were still quite vivid, especially where Uncle Reuben had pinched me.

"Nothing," I said.

"That's far from nothing. You get your clothes on, and you go right to Mrs. Millstein this minute," she ordered.

"But . . ."

"Do what I say," she screamed. She looked horrified as I began to put my school clothes back on. Then she left to go to her office. By the time I arrived at the nurse's office, Mrs. Wilson had called and Mrs. Millstein was waiting, prepared for what she would find.

"Come in, Raven. Please," she said when I opened the door. She had me go into one of the private rooms. "Mrs. Wilson told me about your injuries. Do you want to show them to me?"

"I'm all right," I said.

"I'm sure, but just in case there is something else to do, it might be a good idea to let me see them. Okay?"

I hesitated. And then suddenly, the whole world seemed to come apart for me. I couldn't control myself. The tears that had welled up in my eyes time after time, tears I had driven back or shut off, flooded, poured out of me with no restraint. I began seemingly unstoppable sobbing. Mrs. Millstein had to help me to the chair.

"There, there now, Raven. I'm sure it's not as bad as all that," she said.

"It is," I cried. I lifted my skirt slowly, and she looked at the bruises. Then I stood up, and she examined the others.

"How did this happen, Raven?" she demanded in a firm voice. Again, I hesitated. "You must tell me, Raven. Who did this to you?"

I took a deep breath. Did it matter anymore who knew and what sort of a horrible life I had? I sat again and stared at the floor. The tears dripped off my chin.

"Raven?"

"My uncle," I said in a tired, defeated voice.

"How did he do this?"

"He beat me with a hairbrush," I said, "and he pinched me after . . . after . . ." My tears rushed out again. My chest felt as if it would cave in and crush my heart. Mrs. Millstein fed me tissues and then took my hand.

"Tell me slowly, Raven. Take your time, but tell me everything. I'm here to help you, sweetheart. Go on," she said, kneeling in front of me and holding my hand. "What else did he do to you, honey?"

"After he began to beat me, he touched me

where he shouldn't," I blurted. "Then he hit me with the brush until I nearly fainted."

"Did this happen before?" she asked.

"Yes," I moaned. "Last time, it was with a belt." I started to cry softly.

She stared quietly for a long moment, and then she stood up. "Just rest now, Raven. You're going to be fine," she said. "I'll be right back."

Everything that happened afterward happened so quickly it all blurs together like a movie running too fast in my head. Soon afterward, a woman from the children's protection service, Marjorie Rosner, arrived, and Mrs. Millstein urged me to describe what had happened to me. She questioned me in more detail, and then she and Mrs. Millstein went off to confer. Minutes later, I was escorted out and taken to a doctor who examined my injuries and gave Marjorie Rosner a written report. All the while, things were buzzing around me, telephones ringing, policemen arriving, and then I was taken to a temporary foster home run by an elderly couple. They provided me with a hot meal and a place to sleep. I didn't think I would, but the moment my head hit the pillow, I drifted off, feeling my body sink into the mattress.

In the morning, Marjorie arrived and explained that I was going to a courthouse to be questioned by a family court judge. She warned me that my aunt and my uncle might be in the courthouse as well.

"Your uncle was questioned by the police, as well as your aunt," she told me.

"What about what he said he did to my mother?"

"Let's just concentrate on you for now," Marjorie told me.

I was so frightened I could barely walk to Marjorie's car. She kept reassuring me that everything would be all right.

"He'll never lay a hand on you again, Raven. I promise," she said.

When we entered the courthouse, I saw Aunt Clara sitting alone on a bench in the corridor. She had her head down, her hands in her lap. She looked so small and lost. I felt sorry for her. When she heard us in the hallway, she looked up. Her eyes were bloodshot, her face pale.

"What have you done, Raven?" she asked in a tiny voice.

"It's not what she's done, Mrs. Stack. It's what your husband has done," Marjorie Rosner said.

"He wouldn't do those things," she said. "He wouldn't." She looked up at me hopefully.

"I'm sorry, Aunt Clara. I think you know he would," I said.

Aunt Clara brought her small fist to her mouth to stop the cry that strangled in her throat.

Marjorie moved me ahead. I looked back just before we entered the judge's chambers. Aunt Clara had her hands over her face and was rocking gently on the bench like someone in great pain. My heart felt like a lump of lead.

"I hate hurting her," I said.

"You're doing the right thing, Raven. Just answer the judge's questions," Marjorie said.

I sucked in my breath and stepped in, feeling like someone on a roller coaster who was just reaching the top of another incline. In moments, I knew I would be raging downward, holding on for dear life, closing my eyes, screaming, wondering where the next turn would take me.

Epilogue

Uncle Reuben denied everything, of course. He admitted beating me but claimed that I was so rotten to the core he had no choice. The judge didn't believe him and certainly had no intention of placing me back in Uncle Reuben's home. With my mother gone and no other relatives who could bear responsibility for me, I became a ward of the state. It was what Uncle Reuben had predicted for me all along, so in a way, I suppose he got what he wanted.

I felt sorrier for William and Jennifer, since they had to stay in the home, and told Marjorie so. She thought William eventually might be the one who came out of the family's self-imposed cocoon and eventually helped everyone, especially Aunt Clara.

"In therapy," Marjorie said, "it will all be exposed."

I didn't know whether to believe her or not, and at the moment, I couldn't think about anything else but what was happening to me. She saw how anxious I was and decided she would be the one to bring me to the new foster home herself.

"It's one of our best facilities," she explained the morning she drove me there. "It used to be a small hotel, and the couple who ran the hotel, Gordon and Louise Tooey, now run the home. The grounds are beautiful, and there is lots of room in the building."

She made it sound as if I was going away to summer camp. She said there were other girls my age, and the school I would be attending nearby was one of the better schools in the state.

"Prospective adoptive parents come by frequently, too," she told me.

I didn't know if I wanted another mother. I had never had a father, and my experience with Uncle Reuben made me anxious about being in anyone else's control.

Why would someone come along now to adopt me, anyway? I thought. If I were a woman looking for a child to adopt, I would try to find one who was relatively young, one I could teach and develop. I wouldn't want a daughter who had lived the life I had already lived.

Marjorie saw the pessimism in my face but nevertheless talked continuously about the bright future that awaited me. She promised me that the worst was behind me. She assured me that the state would make sure I was never in the hands of someone as perverted and cruel as my uncle or as troubled as my mother.

"We don't let just anyone take in one of our children," she said, as if the state were a gigantic mother hen with eyes that really saw and examined and knew each and every one of her young chicks.

I was too tired and too depressed to argue or even to care. This would be the third school I would attend in less than six months. There would be new faces, faces with distrustful, cautious eyes. The hardest thing in the world was making a real friend, developing a relationship with another human being who trusted you and cared for you and had confidence that you trusted and cared for her as well. I really never had a friend like that, and now I wondered if I ever would.

A little more than an hour later, we drove up to a place called the Lakewood House. The first thing Marjorie had told me proved to be true. It was a very large building with the biggest wraparound porch I had ever seen. Marjorie helped me with my things and gazed at the grounds. She took a deep breath as if the air was fresher.

"Isn't it beautiful here? Look at the lake back there and the flowers. It's very nice that these people decided to become foster parents and share all this."

Why would they? I wondered.

We started up the steps. There was a screen door, and the door behind it was open. We heard a woman's voice.

"Coming," she cried.

Marjorie opened the screen door, and we faced a tall brunette with shoulder-length hair. She looked about fifty, with vibrant and friendly blue eyes.

"This is Raven Flores," Marjorie said. "Raven, meet Louise Tooey."

"Hi, darlin'," Louise said, reaching for my free hand. "You just come right in. I know all about you," she continued in a soft, sad voice. Her eyes actually became teary. "What we are doing to our children," she remarked to Marjorie, and shook her head. She smiled at me again. "Come on. I'm going to introduce you right away to your roommate. Her name's Brooke, and I'm sure you two will be fast friends. We're like one big family here. We all look out for each other."

I gazed at Marjorie, who nodded and smiled again. I couldn't help being skeptical. I was like the girl who had so many unfulfilled promises that one more just weighed her down deeper into a well of sadness. I'd rather not be promised anything, I thought. Disappointment lingered in the shadows, hungry, eager, ready to pound on my little bit of hope.

"Louise," we heard, and looked up the stairway. "The toilet is running over again."

A tall, thin girl with braces and stringy dark hair looked down at us, her hands on her hips.

"And I wasn't the last one in there," she added quickly. "Please tell Gordon."

"All right, dear. Don't worry. I'll get him." Louise laughed. "They get so nervous when something goes wrong. Gordon fixes everything so quickly. He should. He's been doing it long enough. I'll just take Raven upstairs," she told Marjorie, "and then come down to meet with you in the office."

"Fine. Good-bye, Raven," Marjorie said, hugging me. "You're going to be just fine," she said.

"I don't know why," I said. "I've never been before."

She and Louise exchanged troubled looks, and then I followed Louise up the stairs. The tall girl watched us for a moment before turning to hurry down the corridor. I imagined it was to announce my arrival. We

199

stopped at a room on the left, and Louise knocked.

"Yes?" a voice called.

Louise opened the door.

"It's just Louise, Brooke, with your new roommate that I promised."

"Lucky me," Brooke replied. She looked up from the table upon which she had a tape recorder with its casing apart. It looked as if she was repairing it. When she set eyes on me, however, her head snapped around in a double-take, and she stopped what she was doing.

"This is Raven. Raven, this is Brooke. You two are about the same age, so I imagine you have a lot in common."

"I doubt it," Brooke said.

I smiled at her. "I doubt it, too."

"Oh. Well, Brooke will tell you all about the Lakewood House and introduce you to the other girls on the floor, won't you, Brooke?"

"Do I have a choice?"

"Of course you do, dear."

"Come on," she said in a tired voice. "I'll fill you in on Horror Hotel."

"Brooke!"

"I'm just teasing, Louise. You know that," Brooke said.

"Of course you are. My girls love it here,"

Louise said. "I'll just go finish with Marjorie, and then I'll see you soon after," she told me. "Make yourself at home, dear."

She stepped out, closing the door behind her.

Brooke and I stared at each other a moment.

"You meet Gordon yet?" she asked. I shook my head. "I thought you looked too calm."

"Why? What's he like?"

"He's big, ugly, and mean. Otherwise, he's okay," she said.

I started to smile.

"Haven't you been at other homes?" she asked.

"Just overnight at one. Before that, I've lived with family."

"Family? What happened?"

"It's a long story," I said dryly, "with a bad ending."

"Not yet," Brooke said.

"Excuse me?"

"The ending. It's not written yet."

I shrugged. "What are you doing?"

"Trying to fix Butterfly's tape recorder. Someone dropped it off the stairway. I think I know who."

"Butterfly?"

"She's across the hall with Crystal. You'll

meet them soon. Put your stuff away. You can have half the closet and half the dresser. The bathroom's down the hall."

"Thanks," I said.

"Don't thank me. Thank the state."

She fiddled with the tape recorder as I put things away.

Someone knocked.

"Enter Sesame," Brooke cried, and two girls entered, one small and dainty and the other wearing a pair of glasses with lenses thick as goggles. They both stared at me.

"We heard your roommate arrived," the taller, very intelligent-looking girl said. Her eyes were beady and intense. "I'm Crystal, and this is Janet. We call her Butterfly."

"Hi," Janet said softly. She looked like a doll magically brought to life. Why wouldn't someone have snatched her up by now? I wondered.

"Her name's Raven," Brooke said. "She's had a terrible family life, and she's over-joyed about being brought here."

"Now, don't get her more depressed," Crystal ordered. "We do fine here."

"Sure we do. We're the Three Orphan-teers," Brooke said.

"Now four," Crystal corrected.

Brooke looked at me. "That's up to her," she said.

I laughed. "What was it you said, do I have a choice?"

Brooke laughed. Butterfly beamed a smile, and Crystal shook her head.

"Let's go down and get some slop," Brooke decided, standing.

"Slop?"

"Lunch," Crystal said. "And it's not that bad."

"I like to think of it as bad so I get pleasantly surprised," Brooke said. "Come on."

I started out with them. Crystal fell back.

"It's hard in the beginning," she said, "but you'll see. You get used to it."

"It can't be any worse than where I've been," I said.

She nodded. "That's what we all hope."

She walked faster to take Butterfly's little hand, and we descended.

Out beyond the Lakewood House, in homes across the country, girls our ages were having their lunches, or gathering with friends, or sitting with their families. Their dreams weren't much different from ours. Could anyone look at us and know we had only ourselves now? Was there a look, a gesture, a sound in our voices that betrayed our loneliness?

I did see it in the other three, the distrust, the fear, the hesitation. I supposed that in a real sense, we were sisters, born under the same small and distant star, surrounded by darkness, waiting, watching, desperately trying to keep our light bright.

How many fewer smiles would we have? How many fewer laughs? How many more tears than all the safe and loved girls our ages? What did we do to be brought here to this place?

At the bottom of the stairway, they waited for me to catch up.

"Stick close," Brooke ordered. "You're one of us now."

"I think I've always been," I muttered.

Brooke smiled.

Butterfly looked sad.

Crystal looked thoughtful.

We continued down the hallway, together. Four of us closing ranks, hardening, gathering the strength with which to do battle against loneliness.

Firing up our precious star.

The employees of G.K. Hall hope you have enjoyed this Large Print book. All our Large Print titles are designed for easy reading, and all our books are made to last. Other G.K. Hall books are available at your library, through selected bookstores, or directly from us.

For information about titles, please call:

(800) 257-5157

To share your comments, please write:

Publisher
G.K. Hall & Co.
P.O. Box 159
Thorndike, ME 04986